WAKING
THE
ANCIENTS

CATHERINE CAVENDISH

Praise for *Wrath of the Ancients*

"Like the darkest stories of Poe, Stevenson, and Doyle, it is a slow-burning tale of claustrophobia, madness, secrets, and myths."
– Beauty in Ruins

"The apprehension was so intense that I kept looking up from the book, checking every dark corner in my room, making sure no portraits were staring at me."
– Black Magic Reviews

"If you're looking for a great horror book to read, look no further! *Wrath of the Ancients* has all the ingredients for a spooky tale!
– Mello and June

"An atmospheric gothic horror tale that effortlessly blends together history and the supernatural to create an unsettling horror story that will appeal to almost any horror fan."
– The Horror Bookshelf

"In a world of zombies, vampires and prehistoric sea creatures, *Wrath of the Ancients* is a breath of fresh air."
– 2 Book Lovers' Reviews

"Catherine Cavendish delivers the disquiet and the dread - two things I love."
– Cedar Hollow Reviews

Dedication

For Colin, without whom…

Prologue

The man looked down at his scattered ashes. "I am growing tired of waiting. When will I be free of this prison?"

"Soon." The woman moved away in that fluid, ethereal manner of hers. Her scarlet gown flowed around her. An armlet shaped in the goddess Isis's symbol—a coiled cobra—gleamed. Heavy black kohl rimmed her eyes, emphasizing the deep violet of her irises, while her long, black hair, set in many tight braids, reached her waist. "You must be patient," the woman said. "I told you I would help you get what you desire."

"But that isn't possible. She is back in her body. Back in her tomb."

"All is possible. I have the power. Haven't I proved it? Aren't you the proof of it?"

"I still don't live."

"Your spirit lives."

"My spirit cannot touch her."

"But it can touch her spirit. Mate with her spirit if you so desire."

"And why would you do this for me?"

"My revenge is incomplete. My murdering sister rests while I am forced to wander in spirit with no substance of my own."

"And how will it be done? I am in *your* hands. This is not comfortable for me. I am *always* in control."

The woman threw back her head and laughed, showing black, rotten teeth. Stinking, no doubt, if he could smell anything.

"*You* have not been in control for a long time. The god I serve is Set, and *he* is in control. He will come and he will work through me. More powerful this time, for Sekhmet will bring him."

"And I will have my queen?"

"You will have her."

"She will be in the one who is here now?"

"That is to be determined."

"But *this* one is not of the blood."

"She will not be possessed but transformed. We do not need a blood relative."

"That has been tried before. And failed."

"The rules were not properly followed. You cannot possess *all* of her. You have seen that. The gods will not allow it. Her spirit must be divided. Some of it must remain with her body—and lie cold in her tomb. Waiting. Always waiting. In that way, the gods are appeased, and my price is also exacted."

"So, part of my queen will still wander, looking for her lover, but enough of her spirit will be released to come to me."

"Now you understand. You will have all that you desire, and my revenge will not be compromised."

"And I can be with her. For all time."

The woman didn't answer. She gave the merest hint of a smile and passed on.

In his world of shadows, Dr. Emeryk Quintillus waited.

Chapter 1

Vienna, Austria, 2018

"Count Markus von Dürnstein was the last member of the family to actually live here." The estate agent's English hinted at an expensive education. Barely an inflection to show he was Austrian.

Paula Bancroft smoothed her long, dark hair—a habit she was trying to break. As a child, whenever she had been scared or anxious, this gesture had brought her some comfort. She hadn't done it for years, but this past week, since arriving in Vienna, she had caught herself doing it time and again. It would all be better when she had settled down. Even more so when she had mastered enough of the language to at least get by.

She gazed around at the splendid marble-columned hallway. Recently restored, like the rest of this grand house, it looked fresh, bright, and clinically clean, to a point where its personality had been eradicated.

Paula's husband, Phil, gave her a reassuring wink. "Why don't the family live here anymore?" he asked.

Did she imagine it, or did Stefan—the agent—deliberately avoid eye contact?

"I'm not sure exactly, but I believe they did not wish to stay in Vienna. The family moved to Salzburg more than forty years ago. They have let the house ever since, more or less. It is beautiful, yes?"

Paula nodded. She would definitely have to find some pictures to put on these stark white walls.

"I understand your contract with the United Nations here is for three years?" Stefan asked.

"That's right," Phil replied. "Dream come true, really. I've always loved Vienna. Used to come here a lot when I was a boy. I had relatives here, but they've died now, sadly."

"I am sorry to hear that, Mr. Bancroft."

Phil shrugged. "It was a long time ago. What do you think, Paula? Pretty magnificent, isn't it?"

As long as it isn't all like this, Paula thought. Out loud she said, "Let's have a proper look round."

Stefan smiled. "Of course. We will start with the library." He opened the polished oak door and Paula gasped at the sight ahead of and above her.

"That ceiling is amazing," she said. "It looks like Klimt's work."

Stefan smiled. "You know your art, Mrs. Bancroft. Yes, Gustav Klimt was commissioned to paint this by a former owner, an archeologist called Dr. Emeryk Quintillus. He had a passion for Egyptology, and the painting depicts the arrival of Cleopatra at Tarsus. You see her in her golden barge, attended by her handmaidens. I understand it was painted in around 1905, when Klimt was at the height of his talent. You can tell by all the gold leaf he has used. Of course, you know his most famous painting, *Der Kuss*?"

"*The Kiss?* Yes. It's hanging in the Belvedere Museum, isn't it?"

Stefan nodded. "Along with a number of his paintings. Most galleries in Vienna have their share of Klimt originals."

"I shall make it my job to visit them." Paula tore her eyes away from the opulent queen on her lavish barge. "There must be five thousand books here."

"More, I believe."

"You won't be lost for something to read on the long winter nights when I'm in New York," Phil said.

Paula grimaced. "I'll be a bit stuck until I can speak more German."

"Ah, but Dr. Quintillus—and this is his collection—spoke many languages," Stefan said, "including fluent English. I believe he spent some years working at Oxford University. The books in English are up on the second level. You go up the staircase." Stefan indicated a wrought iron spiral stairway in the corner of the room.

"Was Dr. Quintillus a relation of the von Dürnsteins?" Paula asked. "I was wondering why all his books are still here."

"No, he doesn't seem to have had any relatives. When he died, I understand the house was briefly occupied but then left empty for some years, until it was bought by an uncle of Count Markus. He mysteriously disappeared one night, along with his wife. It is a strange story. They were never seen again and, having no children, the house passed to his nephew as next of kin. Through every change of occupant, the books stayed. It is quite a collection."

"It certainly is. I shall enjoy myself in here." Paula pictured herself spending many happy hours surrounded by what promised to be an eclectic collection of literature.

"Come on, let's see the rest of the house," Phil said. "You'll have all the time you want to spend in here, but Stefan will have to get back to the office."

Paula reluctantly allowed herself to be led out of the library and into room after room, all furnished with traditional, dark wood furniture. A dining room with a long, polished mahogany table and eight chairs, a living room with wood-block floor, thick-pile red rugs and a comfortable-looking suite. A massive flat-screen TV mounted on one wall and an open fire stacked with sweet-smelling pine logs promised cozy nights curled up with a glass of Blaufränkisch wine.

On the next floor, corridors led off either side of the staircase, and Stefan opened one door after the other. Most of the rooms stood empty. Three contained contemporary furniture and comfy-looking double or king-sized beds.

"This one has traditionally been used as the master bedroom." Stefan opened the door and, for a second, Paula caught a faint whiff of lilies. Gone as soon as it had appeared, she dismissed it. Furniture polish, probably. Goodness knew there was certainly plenty of polishing to be done, especially downstairs. Still, she had been promised some help. She might not have a job here, but she certainly didn't intend to swap the life of a history teacher for one of a domestic housewife.

She tested the bed with her hand and sat down on it. "We should sleep well on this," she said. "The mattress is good and firm."

Phil picked up a fluffy white pillow. "And we can have pillow fights." He threw it at her and she ducked. It flew over her head and landed on the floor.

Out of the corner of her eye, Paula caught Stefan giving them an odd look. No doubt he wasn't used to seeing forty-somethings playing and giggling like schoolkids. Paula stood, and Phil retrieved the pillow.

"You will see the room has been recently decorated," Stefan pointed at the walls. "I hope you like the color. I chose it myself."

"Very nice," Paula said, not totally sure she liked the gray in so much abundance in a bedroom. It seemed more in keeping with a living room, but she could live with it.

"Love the carpet." She stroked it with her foot. Soft, thick pile, with a contemporary design in shades of gray and lilac.

"The en suite is through here." Stefan opened a door and snapped on the light. Paula took in the stunning black-and-white marble walls and the generous sized bath. Ideal for a luxurious, long soak.

A shadow flitted across the periphery of her vision. She shivered. Her eyes must be playing tricks on her.

"You cold?" Phil asked, joining her. He put his arm around her.

"No. I don't know why I did that. You know that old saying—a goose just walked over my grave? Well, it felt like that. *Seriously* like that."

"Apart from random wandering wild fowl, what do you think of Villa Dürnstein?"

"I like it." Paula told herself she meant it, but somewhere deep inside her, the same instinct that had made her shiver now began to worry at her. She dismissed it.

"What's on the top floor?" she asked.

Stefan looked surprised she had posed that particular question. But surely anyone would be curious?

"Just more rooms. Originally the servants lived up there. I believe it is all empty now. You can use it for storage, or maybe put anything you don't require in one of the spare rooms on this floor."

"It seems such a shame," Paula said. "I mean, a lovely big house and only the two of us rattling around. A place like this should have a large family, loads of kids running up and down these corridors."

She hadn't imagined it. The estate agent flinched when she said that. In that moment, she was sure he knew something he wasn't telling them—and that thought bothered her more than a little.

"When we arrived, I noticed there were windows below street level," she said. "So there's a basement, right?"

"Yes, there is a basement. The old kitchen is down there. About forty years ago, the family installed a new kitchen in one of the rooms on the ground floor. For modern convenience, of course. You wouldn't like your food to get cold."

"Of course." Paula was beginning to dislike this man. He was too smooth, and right now she wouldn't have trusted him to direct her in a straight line. "I'd like to go down there, please."

"Paula!" Phil said. "Now? Really? You can explore all the nooks and crannies when we've moved in, surely."

Paula shot him a look. "I'd like to investigate now, while Stefan is still here. That way if anything's wrong, or we have any questions, we can get them answered straight away."

"Well, I suppose that makes some sort of sense," Phil said. "Stefan, would you mind?"

Again, the oily smoothness dripped off him. Yet it didn't seem to bother Phil at all.

"Not at all," Stefan said. "I would show you down there if I could." A hint of a smile played around the corners of his lips. Paula didn't like that smile. Sly. She guessed what was coming next.

"The problem is," he said, "I don't have a key to the basement. I am not sure if my company has one, either. No one has ever asked to go down there."

"Really?" Paula couldn't remove all trace of sarcasm from her voice. Phil looked at her questioningly. "I would have thought anyone living here would want to get to know every inch of it. It's an intriguing old house, and basements are usually where you find the most interesting bits. All the forgotten detritus. This one has the added advantage of housing an old kitchen, presumably with at least some of the original utensils and cooking devices still intact. I would find that fascinating."

"My wife paints. She's an artist." Paula wished Phil didn't sound as if he was attempting to explain her reaction.

"Then you are in the right city, Mrs. Bancroft. Have you exhibited yet?"

Before Paula could respond, Phil chipped in. "She's won prizes for her paintings and sold a few."

"It's a hobby of mine. I like to paint landscapes and interesting buildings. That's why I'm so interested in the basement."

"Yes, I can understand that. Wait until you see the garden. You will want to paint that, I am sure."

Paula smiled at him but was determined not to let Stefan off lightly. "When do you think you would be able to locate a key?"

Again, his eyes avoided her. There was no mistaking it this time. What was he hiding?

"I'm not sure. I will have to contact the family. Maybe it is lost."

"If that's the case, we'll need to get a locksmith in and have the lock changed. That won't be a problem, will it?" She smiled, determined to match his smoothness with her own.

Stefan said nothing. Phil frowned. "Come on, let's get back to the hotel. Our trunks will be arriving here tomorrow and we need an early start."

They made their way downstairs, and Stefan handed Phil the keys. Paula returned to the library for one last look at Klimt's painting. "Dr. Quintillus," she said. "Who were you, I wonder?"

It happened again. The briefest of movements, glimpsed for a split second. Nothing there now, but she was sure a shadow had flitted across the wall, exactly like upstairs. Stefan and Phil stood by the door, open to the street. Sounds of cars, buses, and the clang of a tram filtered in from outside, along with a chilly draft that reminded her that, spring might be here, but winter wasn't quite ready to let go.

"Let us know when you find that key," Paula said to Stefan.

"Certainly, Madame." He gave her the briefest of nods. She could imagine him clicking his heels in true Teutonic fashion. It brought a smile to her lips and a giggle she fought to suppress.

Phil took her arm as they strolled down the street to the tram stop. "What was all that about?"

"What?"

"You know perfectly well. That basement business."

"He's hiding something. Surely you could see that."

Phil laughed. "Oh yeah, sure. Bodies in the basement."

"No, seriously. I didn't like him. He was oily. Too ingratiating."

"Oh, he was all right. A bit over the top maybe."

"I can't understand what the deal is. Why we're evidently not supposed to go down to the basement. If there's nothing there, why bother locking it?"

"Maybe it's unsafe or something. I mean, if it hasn't been used in decades, all sorts of nasties could be lurking down there. Dry rot, worm-eaten timbers. Anything."

"Maybe." They arrived at their stop. A tram rolled toward them. "That's something I love about Vienna," Paula said, as it pulled up and the doors slid open. "The public transport. Always a tram when you want one."

"Told you you'd love it here." Phil followed her up the step.

"I'll love it even more when I've seen that basement," she said, settling herself in a double seat. Phil sat next to her and she winked at him. "It's going to be an exciting three years."

"Exciting in a good way, I hope." Phil squeezed her hand.

———

Phil slammed his hand down hard on the dining table. "I don't see what the big deal is, Paula. You heard Stefan. He called the family and they're adamant they don't want anyone going down into that basement. Now let it go. Please."

Paula was tempted to protest. Ever since she was a child, she had been fascinated by old houses, especially the kitchens, with their gleaming copper pans and old-fashioned cooking ranges. Now that she had the potential to explore one in her own house, she couldn't let the opportunity pass. Besides, the urge to pick up her brushes and paint again had been biting at her for ages. That old kitchen, untouched for decades, would provide the perfect subject.

"I think it's strange that they'd be so bothered. It makes me wonder what's down there, that's all."

"You read too many crime novels."

"I haven't read one in years. Besides, I have Dr. Quintillus's collection to get through."

Phil smiled. His anger was usually short lived, and today proved no exception. A quick flash and then over. He glanced at his watch. "Hell, I'm going to be late. I've got a meeting at ten."

He grabbed his suit jacket from where he had draped it over the chair, retrieved his briefcase and, after delivering a quick peck to Paula's cheek, left. The rest of the day stretched out before Paula. No German lesson today. She should practice some vocabulary and grammar ahead of a short test, but that would keep for an hour or two. She had finally sorted out their possessions, which had crowded their small apartment in London, but were swallowed by the vastness of this house.

Now it was time to explore the top floor.

She mounted the stairs up to the first floor and then took the next flight up to the former servants' quarters. Hardly a sound penetrated from outside, only the occasional car horn or police siren. Paula walked down the corridor. Her footsteps echoed on the bare boards. She opened one door after the other, each revealing an empty room. Evidently, redecoration had stopped at the floor below. It made sense, though. What would be the point if no one was going to live up here? Paula felt a pang of guilt. Such a waste of a big house. They could have lived in a much smaller apartment for the same money but, as Phil had reasoned, why miss out on such an amazing place? It had been ridiculously cheap by Viennese standards. By any standards, really. Presumably the von Dürnstein family didn't need the money, but wanted the house to be lived in. They certainly signed the contract quickly enough.

The last door Paula came to was at the far end of the corridor. She had to put her shoulder to it. A series of reluctant creaks echoed off the walls until it finally let her in.

An old, worn rug lay haphazardly across bare floorboards. A neat, old-fashioned fireplace, containing a small quantity of ancient ashes, and a single bed covered in a dusty quilt were the only signs of former habitation. Paula wondered why she tiptoed into the room. Why not just stride in there?

Because it doesn't feel right.

She made her way to the window and looked out over the street to the rear wall of the Schönbrunn Palace. The trees were newly green with their spring leaves. That would make a pleasant view for anyone waking up in this room.

A faint whiff of lilies drifted by. Paula sniffed. She caught her breath. Footsteps. A floorboard creaked. She spun round. Held her breath. Listened.

The door slowly closed, making whispering creaks as it moved. She watched, fascinated. How could it do that when it had been so stiff earlier? Maybe she was standing on an unstable floorboard. She moved to her right. Still, the door inched its slow way closed. Paula didn't wait any longer. She crossed the small room in a second, yanked the door wide open, glanced each way down the empty corridor and sped off toward the stairs, her heart beating drumrolls.

The door slammed as she made it to the bottom stair on the first floor. Breathing hard, she raced to the bedroom she shared with Phil. Once inside, she shut the door tightly and sank down onto the bed, clutching the duvet with shaking hands.

She struggled to calm her breathing, forcing herself to take deep breaths while she wrestled with what had just happened.

It's an old house. Old houses creak. The floor's probably uneven and the door swings shut naturally. As for the footsteps…maybe I imagined them.

It all made perfect sense. If only Paula could accept it. If only she could stop shaking.

She must calm down. She stood and made for the en suite. The soft light revealed her terrified, pale face. Paula ran cold water over her wrists and hands and patted her cheeks. Drying herself with the towel, she switched off the light and turned back. She stopped. A shadow. That split-second smell of lilies. Gone almost before she could recognize it.

Nothing moved. The only sound in the double-glazed room came from an ornate mantelpiece clock that gave a steady, gentle tick.

Paula shook her head. *Get a grip, woman.* Those footsteps and that door upstairs had spooked her. Footsteps? There couldn't have been any. Just old floorboards and house timbers settling. Her imagination had filled in the rest and, God knows, she'd never been short of *that*.

Coffee. That would fix her. Fresh Viennese coffee. Strong, black, sweet. Perfect.

She ground her coffee, loaded the coffee maker and the irresistible aroma soon filled the kitchen. While she waited, she inspected the door leading to the basement. With two padlocks and a mortice lock, there must be not one but three different keys. But Stefan had clearly stated that the family wasn't prepared to let him have the *key*. Singular. Maybe she was reading too much into this, but she couldn't shift the feeling that the estate agent hadn't told them the whole truth. Had he even *phoned* the family?

She took her coffee into the library and contemplated lighting the wood fire. The big room had a high ceiling, and the central heating only took the edge off the chill. Paula set her mug down and went over to the fireplace. She and Phil had basked in the glow of the firelight a couple of chilly evenings ago and she had re-laid the fire the following morning. She reached for the box of long matches that rested on the mantel, struck one, and in a few minutes was toasting her stockinged feet and sipping her coffee.

The fresh pine smell of the logs warmed her, and the heat cocooned her so that her eyes grew heavy. Finishing her coffee, she leaned back in the chair and closed her eyes. As she drifted off to sleep, she heard the crackle, hiss, and spit of the logs, and felt soothed. Her earlier fears faded into the distance.

She floated along a gentle river she could neither see nor feel. It lapped the banks on either side of her. They too were hidden in the inky blackness that surrounded her. Shadowy figures, indistinct and unfamiliar to her, drifted in and out of her vision. One loomed closer. The nearer it came, the more apprehensive she grew. She could make out that the shadow was male, growing ever more tangible the closer it got. It stared at her, its bearded face framed by long, dark hair. A stovepipe hat and long Edwardian-style coat completed the picture. So close now she could reach out and touch…what? A ghost?

The figure smiled at her, but she could read no joy in that smile — only emptiness. Paula stared at the face. She was being drawn closer. Any second now, and she would be consumed.

The figure spoke in her mind. *You are mine. You have always been mine.*

Paula screamed herself awake.

"Oh my God. What the hell...?" She grasped the arms of her chair and stood. She stared around the room, to the upper level and along the narrow walkway. She was alone. So why did she feel eyes watching her?

The ceiling. That painting of Cleopatra. It seemed so alive. And there was something else. Something she hadn't noticed before, although she had lost count of the number of times she had studied it over the past few days.

In one corner of the painting, a female figure watched the proceedings. In profile, she bore a slight resemblance to Cleopatra. Maybe Klimt had used the same model for both roles. Perhaps he had meant her to resemble someone closely related to the queen. Paula focused her attention on the new subject. The figure was dressed in a deep red gown, made of material so fine it clung to every curve of her slim form. Her arms were bare and on the one fully visible, she wore an armlet of an entwined golden snake. Her left hand clutched at some reeds that were growing on the riverbank where she stood. Paula struggled to make out her expression from her profile, but the heavily kohl-rimmed eye and the set of her jaw gave Paula the impression of anger. Hatred, even. Threat. Paula shivered. Klimt managed to convey strong emotion so powerfully, and in this painting, with this minor figure, he had excelled himself. She couldn't look at it anymore and turned away.

A memory stirred. She had studied ancient Egyptian history but hadn't taught it for years. Cleopatra. There had been a sister, or a half-sister. Arsinoe. There had been no love lost and a lot of rivalry between the two. Cleopatra had rightly perceived her sister as a threat to her monarchy and had her firstly banished to a temple in Ephesus, Turkey, and then murdered on its steps. Could Arsinoe be the minor figure in the painting?

Somewhere in this vast library that had once belonged to an archeologist—especially one with such a fascination with Egyptology—there would surely be at least one book on Egypt's most famous queen. Paula began her search. She ran her finger along a shelf. Judging by the dust, no one had touched these books since their former owner. They were arranged by subject matter. Many in German, some in languages Paula could only guess at. Hungarian possibly, or one of the Balkan tongues. When she found the right section, book after book featured titles on Egypt. She searched among them, scanning the shelves until she located one in English. *A Life of Cleopatra*. She flipped the pages and found the index. There were half a dozen references to Arsinoe, and she sat down to read them.

Five minutes later, she knew little more than she had at the beginning. Arsinoe was a footnote in history. A troublesome, power-hungry menace who was murdered, probably at the age of around twenty. Cleopatra could have reasonably pleaded self-defense, because all the references agreed Arsinoe had plans to shorten her sister's life considerably. Paula replaced the book on the shelf and looked back at the painting.

Cleopatra stared down at her, and Paula noticed the coldness of her eyes. The full, sensual lips and jet-black hair, her white, flowing dress and the glittering gold of her barge—a painting in which, every time you looked at it, you seemed to see something new. Like the ankh Cleopatra wore on the belt of her dress. Paula had never noticed that before. But now another thought troubled her.

The image of the frightening man she had dreamed about flashed into her mind. She must get him down on paper while the details were still fresh. She opened the wide drawer in the desk and withdrew her sketching pad and pencils. She could picture him so vividly that within ten minutes, her drawing had already taken shape. A few minutes more and the sinister face looked back at her. Paula smiled at the irony of that. How could he stare?

He had no eyes.

The cheekbones were pronounced, his face bearded and his hair long, black and flowing. The two black holes where his eyes should have been dominated her drawing. Paula shivered and pushed the sketch pad aside.

Thank God it was only a dream.

The mantel clock chimed twelve. Time to make a sandwich for lunch, then tackle those verbs and practice pronunciation. Frau Schmidt had the ability to make her exclusively adult pupils feel six years old again—especially if they hadn't done their homework. Besides, Paula would be here alone for some weeks. Phil was being sent to New York to cover for a colleague and sort out some problems. If she could speak the language better, she could feel more a part of this elegant cultural city that was now—for a time at least—her home.

"I knew you'd have to go to New York at some stage, maybe towards the end of this year, but I never thought you'd have to go so quickly." Paula took a sip of Burgenland red wine but barely registered it.

The fire crackled in the living room. Phil wandered over, her sketch pad in his hand. "They're in a mess over there. It's what I'm paid to sort out." He pointed at her latest drawing. "He's a bit evil-looking. Anyone you know?"

"A stupid nightmare I had. It was so vivid I wanted to get it down on paper. I thought I might use it somehow, but now I'm not so sure."

"Why not? It's a very unusual image."

"Not my usual style, though. He looks like something out of a horror film."

"So? You don't always have to paint landscapes and interiors. Branch out a bit. You're in Vienna now. Home of Gustav Klimt and the Secessionists. Follow their example and break the mold."

Paula smiled. Phil sat beside her and put the sketch pad on her knee. Paula glimpsed the face and placed the pad face down on the settee next to her.

"I wish you didn't have to go so soon. I know it's not for a week or two, but we've only just arrived here."

Phil slipped his hand into hers. "I know it's not ideal, but they're really struggling, with two staff away on long-term sick and a third going on maternity leave. It's only for three weeks or so. Give you a chance to get to know Vienna, and no distractions from your German lessons."

Paula pinched his nose. "Funny guy. Well, think of me all alone in this great big house with only the ghosts for company."

"Ghosts?"

"Just an expression. I hope. Anyway, the cleaner is starting in a couple of weeks, so I'll have someone to talk to."

"Anna. She's Spanish, isn't she?"

"Italian. Anna Manchetti. She comes from Tuscany, not far from Florence, and she's studying English at the university here. She seems levelheaded and conscientious. We should get on well."

Phil stroked her hand, a look of concern in his eyes. "You'll be all right, won't you? Here on your own?"

"Of course I will. I'm a big girl, and this house will keep me busy. I haven't finished getting it how I want it yet. I need more pictures for the walls. I'll have plenty to do while you're away."

"Well, if you need me, I'll be on the other end of a phone and we'll Skype every evening—evening my time, that is. It'll be after midnight for you."

Paula smiled. "I always was a night owl." Being alone in a house had never bothered her. Before she and Phil got together, she used to live on her own in a sizable flat in a large, converted house built in the seventeenth century. Plenty of fodder for ghost stories there. So why should the prospect of being on her own here for a few weeks trouble her? Yet, butterflies dive-bombed inside her stomach, and she wished with all her heart Phil wasn't going away.

Paula woke early. The first rays of sunlight penetrated the clouds, promising a warm spring day. She showered, washed her hair, and dressed in jeans and a plain T-shirt, then donned flat strappy sandals and padded quietly out of the bedroom where Phil continued to sleep.

Out in the garden, she inhaled the scent of fresh damp grass. Dew lay on the lawn, and in the flower borders, red and gold tulips intertwined with daffodils and harebells. Birds sang from the tree branches and Paula hugged herself and smiled. She and Phil had landed a wonderful assignment here. Okay, so she couldn't get into the basement—yet. But this place inspired her. As she had said to Phil, she had plenty to keep her occupied.

The sun glinted off something shiny and metallic lying in a flower bed.

Paula stepped over to it, bent down and picked it up. An old-fashioned cigarette lighter. Silver, by the weight of it. She turned it over in her hand and found two elaborately engraved initials. *E.Q.*

"Emeryk Quintillus," she whispered.

A breeze as soft as a sigh stroked her hair. But not a leaf stirred.

She slid the lighter into the pocket of her jeans and strolled back in through the kitchen door, deep in thought.

Phil was making coffee. "You're up early."

"It's such a perfect morning. I felt like getting some air, and the garden is so lovely and peaceful. Look, I found this."

She fished out the lighter and handed it to Phil. He put down the coffee mugs and took it from her. He flipped the top and tried to strike it. "Flint's gone." He shook it. "Empty. Nice looking thing, though. Make an attractive ornament."

"I'll put it on the mantel in the library. Maybe we could get it fixed sometime."

"Not much point if we don't smoke."

Paula opened the library door and crossed the room to the fireplace. She stood the lighter on the mantel and stepped back. Her sketch pad lay where she had left it on the settee. She would want that later, so she picked it up. Instantly, she was confronted by the drawing of the man in her nightmare.

But this couldn't be right.

"Phil," she called as she sped out of the library, back into the kitchen, sketch pad in hand.

"What's up?"

"Look at this. I didn't draw that. Well, I drew *some* of it, but not all that."

Phil peered at the drawing. "What am I looking for?"

"Don't you see? I only drew a face, eyes, that long hair. Now he's got a right hand...fingers...and he's smoking a cigar, I think, or something like it."

"And you say that wasn't on the picture you drew yesterday?"

"You *know* it wasn't. You saw it."

Phil handed the pad back to Paula. "I'm really sorry, but I don't remember how much detail was on that picture. I remember the face, but that's about it."

"But...you *must* remember."

"Sorry. I don't. Right now, I've got to get to work. Busy day." He kissed the still stunned Paula on the lips and left her.

She stared at the picture. Could she have drawn all this detail and simply forgotten? The hand that held the slim cigar to the man's lips revealed long, slender fingers. An artist's hand, perhaps. Paula examined her own. Phil had told her he had fallen in love with her hands first and then the rest of her. She had never known whether he really meant it, but it didn't matter. She had fallen in love with his eyes, and the crazy way his hair would flop over them. It didn't now, of course. Now he worked for the United Nations, it was suits, ties and smart haircuts all the way.

The picture bothered her more and more the longer she looked at it. It would have to go. She ripped it off the pad and, without thinking, reached for the lighter she had found earlier.

She flicked open the top and struck it. A blue flame shot up and she touched the paper to it. As it burned, she dropped it in the fireplace and watched it shrivel, blacken and disintegrate into ashes. Paula replaced the lighter and suddenly remembered.

The lighter didn't work. So how...?

She rubbed a clammy palm against her jeans and hesitantly retrieved the lighter. She shook it. Nothing. She struck it. Nothing. She threw it back on the mantel and backed away from it. In the fireplace, the last of the embers from the burned paper died away.

Her skin prickled.

―――――

"It couldn't have, Paula." Phil stabbed a roast potato.

"I'm telling you it did. I had the shock of my life when I realized."

"Lighters don't work with no fuel and no flint."

"You explain it then. You've seen the ashes in the fireplace. How did they get there if not the way I said?"

Phil shrugged. "How should I know? Look, Paula, are you sure you're all right? Maybe it's the move…all the upheaval…"

"I'm fine. *I'm* not the problem. It's that bloody lighter."

Phil set his knife and fork down and laid his hand over hers. "Okay, I confess I don't have an explanation for it, but just put it down to some weird quirk. Get rid of the lighter if it bothers you so much."

"I might just do that. Sell it on eBay or something. It might be worth a bit."

"Good idea. Now, how about we go down to the bar we went to last week? There's a good crowd there and you can practice your German."

Paula smiled, but an uncomfortable feeling that she couldn't explain made her stomach lurch.

During the next few days, Paula felt less spooked. The lighter had disappeared from the mantel. Phil must have put it somewhere or taken it away altogether. She meant to mention it to him but kept forgetting. No matter.

She kept seeing the locked basement door, but despite her best efforts, Stefan had still not come up with any news of keys. Phil came home tired every night and she had never been a nagging wife. If necessary, she would wait until he had left for New York before tackling the estate agent on her own.

She made daily trips into the city, taking her sketch pad with her. Statues of Johann Strauss and Franz Schubert provided excellent subjects for her attention, and she spent happy hours sitting on one of the many benches in the Stadtpark, her pencil flying across the sheet.

A few days before Phil's departure for New York, she came home from a morning's sketching and set her pad down on the library table. Her hair felt clammy, and she wiped her face with a tissue. It had been like a summer day. Hot sun, cloudless sky. In the fridge she would find a bottle of iced lemon tea. She went off to get it, returning a few minutes later.

She picked up her sketchbook to examine the morning's work, flipped through the earlier pages and stopped dead.

The face stared out at her. This time, he had eyes. Deeply disturbing, menacing eyes. The face had the beard she recognized, the long hair, and on his head, a stovepipe hat. The portrait, sketched with her pencil, showed head and shoulders only and its subject appeared to be wearing a jacket, shirt and elaborate cravat.

Paula pushed the pad away, her heart pounding. Let Phil explain that away.

"You must have drawn it. It's in your style." Phil handed the pad back to Paula, who could hardly bare to touch it. She threw it down on the library desk.

"If I did, how is it I don't remember?"

"I can't answer that. Perhaps you need to see a doctor."

"I'm not ill."

"Well..." He indicated the drawing.

"Won't you even consider the possibility that something odd is going on here? I know you took the lighter away—"

"I never touched the damned lighter."

"It's not on the mantel."

"Then *you* must have moved it."

"I didn't."

Phil ran his hands through his hair. "This is getting us nowhere. I don't want to argue with you, Paula. I'm going away for a few weeks and I'd hate us to part like this."

Paula bit her tongue. He was right. Infuriating. But right. Somewhere there had to be a rational explanation for this. God knew where, but somewhere.

She bit back the angry words that threatened to spew out of her. "Righteous anger," some might call it. If only they could get through the next few days without incident. Meanwhile, she would buy a new sketch pad. She didn't think she would ever be able to use that one again.

————

Seeing Phil off at the airport, Paula gave him one last wave, heaved a sigh, and turned to go. She took the City Airport Train into the center of the city and the Underground speeded her back to Hietzing. In the small town center, she bought cheeses, fresh bread, fruit and vegetables, selected a bottle of Sekt, and walked back home, deep in thought.

Her new sketchpad lay on the kitchen table—the old one, with its inexplicable drawing, consigned to the drawer of the library desk. As far as she was concerned, it could stay there forever, as long as she didn't have to look at that awful face again.

————

Anna Manchetti was roughly Paula's height of five feet six inches, slim with long black hair tied back in a flowing ponytail. Her deep brown eyes shone as she smiled at Paula on the doorstep.

"Pleased to meet you," she said, her voice pleasantly accented.

"And you. Come in. I'll show you around."

Anna followed Paula into the hall. "It is beautiful here."

Paula nodded. "Yes. I'll show you the library. It's through here."

Paula opened the door and Anna drew a sharp intake of breath as she stepped over the threshold.

"The painting. It's magnificent."

"A Gustav Klimt original. Commissioned by the then owner, an archeologist called Dr. Emeryk Quintillus."

Anna gave a quick start. "This was Emeryk Quintillus's house?"

"Yes." Paula saw the color drain from the girl's face. "Why? Is there a problem?"

"N-no. Just…" She shook her head. "I have heard of him from a friend at university. There are stories about this house and Dr. Quintillus. He was a very strange man. Eccentric, I think is the right word. He was in love with Cleopatra."

Paula pointed up at the painting. "This Cleopatra?"

"Yes, he was convinced he could find her tomb. He went to Egypt many times, collecting pieces for various museums. Then he disappeared. No one really knows what happened to him. Some say he still haunts this house." She looked as if she wished she hadn't said that.

"How strange. I wonder if he ever found her."

"I don't think so. They are still looking, aren't they?"

"Ah, well. Thank you for telling me about him. He certainly left his mark on this house. All these books were his, too."

Anna sniffed. "Do you have any lilies in the house?"

"No, but it's funny you should say that. Now and again I swear I can smell them. I thought it was furniture polish at first, but I couldn't find any that smelled like that."

Anna sneezed. "Sorry. I'm allergic. I always sneeze whenever I am anywhere near them." She sneezed again and fished a new tissue out of a packet in her purse. "I'm so sorry."

"Please, don't apologize."

Anna blew her nose and sniffed again. "It's gone now." She replaced the tissue in her purse and smiled at Paula. "I should start my work."

"Right. I'll show you where everything is in the kitchen."

With Anna happy to polish all the furniture downstairs, Paula took dusters and bathroom cleaner upstairs to clean their bedroom and en suite. As she passed the stairs leading up to the top floor, a cold draft chilled her. Had she left a window open the other day when she had been up there? Strange she hadn't felt it before now.

Memories of her earlier experience up there warned her off, but she decided she had better investigate. She couldn't leave the upstairs unsecured, so she mounted the staircase. At the top, she looked along the corridor of closed doors. She moved steadily along, opening each one, entering and inspecting the locked windows, until she came to the only room with any furniture. Sure enough, the window was open. She went over to it, shut and locked it.

The door slammed.

Paula dashed over and turned the handle. It creaked its protesting way open as she tugged. She hadn't needed to work so hard on the previous occasion when the door had started to shut. Now she could swear someone was pulling in the opposite direction. She dismissed the thought. Preposterous.

It suddenly gave, throwing her backward. A cold breeze tickled her ear. Paula turned and saw the window, once again ajar.

But I shut it.

She retraced her steps over to the window and pulled it firmly shut, twisting the window lock tightly. In the fireplace, the ashes stirred, making a faint noise, like the crackling of dry leaves.

A sigh echoed off the walls. Paula raced out of the room and made to close the door. It slammed shut in her face. She gave an involuntary cry, charged back down the stairs and met Anna in the hallway.

"Mrs. Bancroft, what has happened? You look as if you have had a terrible fright."

Paula concentrated on breathing steadily, but her words tumbled out in a rush. "A door upstairs keeps slamming. The window was open, so I closed it. But it opened again. By itself. I know it sounds stupid… It couldn't have, could it? I must have made it happen, but for the life of me I don't know how." Paula's teeth were chattering from shock.

Anna set down the mop and bucket she had been using to clean the hall floor.

"Come into the kitchen. I'll make you a cup of sweet tea."

"Thank you. Coffee. I'd prefer coffee, please. I'm not a great tea drinker."

Minutes later, Anna handed her a cup of steaming coffee. Paula took it gratefully and sipped.

Anna frowned, as if she didn't know whether to tell her something.

Paula set her cup down. She felt calmer now. Back in control. "If you've got any ideas about what just happened, now's the time to share them." She gave a wry smile. "All explanations welcome."

Anna hesitated a moment longer. "It's just that… My friend told me some stories about this house. Strange stories. I never thought I would ever come to Dr. Quintillus's house, and, because of these stories, I was relieved."

Paula braced herself. "Go on. You can't stop now. Tell me what your friend told you."

Chapter 2

Phil stared back at her from her phone screen on their daily Skype call. "You don't mean to say you believe her? Ghosts roaming around at night? Ancient Egyptian curses?" He laughed. "She's winding you up."

In the library, with the homely sounds of a crackling fire and the gentle ticking of the clock, Paula felt inclined to agree. If only she could.

"I know it sounds crazy, and it's probably all urban myth, but some odd things have been happening around here. I can check up on at least one of the stories. Anna told me there was an English secretary — Adeline Ogilvy. Just before the First World War, she came over here to type up Dr. Quintillus's memoirs. She ended up in a care home in London where, according to Anna, she was literally frightened to death. Okay, maybe that's a bit exaggerated. But I bet, with a little effort, I could trace this Adeline."

"She'll be long dead now, surely. Anyway, I thought the house had been in the von Dürnstein family for generations?"

"They sold it back in 1977, shortly before the count passed on, but bought it back after the new owner died in some crazy fire. Anna told me the family were scared it would fall into the wrong hands again, whatever that might mean. There's something else, though. The basement."

"What about it?"

"After Markus von Dürnstein inherited the house, he had considerable problems when he began work opening up some previously walled-up rooms. Eventually no workmen in Vienna or the surrounding area would come near the place. Then, for some reason, he had the rooms down there walled up again. He was the one who decided on a new kitchen up on the ground floor and also the one who decreed that the door down to the basement should be permanently locked and that, under no circumstances, was any tenant to be given the keys."

"But they would have to be handed over to the new owner when they sold it."

"Yes, they were. And look what happened to her."

Phil sighed. "I think you'd better stop asking Anna any more questions about the house. She's clearly got a wealth of tall stories. You know how these things build up. Like Chinese whispers. Everyone adds their own little touch when they retell the story."

Paula fought the urge to snap at him. She hated it on the rare occasions when he saw fit to make her feel incapable of rational thought. An unintentional habit, for sure. But an annoying one. She concentrated on keeping her voice steady.

"I know exactly what you mean, but my curiosity has got the better of me and I intend to contact the care home in London."

"You know which one it was?" Phil sounded surprised. His eyebrows had done that funny lopsided rise of his.

"I know Adeline Ogilvy lived in Wimbledon. Once I've eliminated the residential-only homes and focused on those that also provide nursing care, it shouldn't take long."

"You don't even know if they're still in business. When did she die?"

"1980."

Phil shrugged. "Wild geese spring to mind."

"I know I could draw a blank, but I really want to try. Then we'll see how much of the legend of this place is fact and how much fantasy…at least on that score. Aren't you the least bit curious?"

"Frankly, Paula, I'm too knackered. I put in a fourteen-hour day yesterday and the same today. If you want to do this, knock yourself out. How's the German coming along?"

"*Ganz gut, danke.*"

"Keep it up. How's Frau Frankenstein?"

Paula laughed. "Schmidt. I reckon she puts on the dragon act. I'll bet, deep inside, she's a marshmallow."

Phil laughed. "I'm going to have to go. If I don't get some sleep soon, I'll be no good tomorrow and it's wall-to-wall meetings all day."

"Night, Phil. Love you."

"Night, Paula."

He ended the call and Paula settled down to read, quickly losing herself in her latest book from Quintillus's collection, *The Island of Dr. Moreau* by H.G. Wells. Sometime later, yawning, she closed the book. She had lost track of time and now it was two a.m. and the fire had died down to a red glow. She moved around the room, turning off lamps. Before switching off the last one under the painting, she paused to look up at it. Her attention was drawn to the figure on the bank. Something seemed different about her tonight.

With a start, Paula realized what it was. Instead of reeds, the girl was clutching a gleaming gold dagger.

Chapter 3

Paula backed out of the room and slammed the door. She leaned against the polished wood, panting. The room was dim. Her eyes had played tricks on her. She must have imagined the figure was holding a dagger. Paintings don't change. A nerve in her temple throbbed. She massaged it and made for the kitchen. A cup of tea. That might calm her. The only time she ever drank tea was late at night when coffee would keep her awake.

The sickly smell hit her as she switched on the light. The distinctive, oversweet aroma of lilies. Now it came over much stronger than before. As if someone had put a vaseful of them somewhere in the room. Paula looked all around but saw nothing out of place. Still, the unwelcome scent lingered, heavy and cloying, nauseating.

The closer she got to the basement door, the stronger the smell. It seemed to be wafting through the keyhole. Hesitantly, Paula crouched down and put her eye to the small hole, but there was only blackness on the other side. She stared for a few seconds, but the unrelenting darkness revealed nothing.

She straightened up and the smell vanished as suddenly as it had struck.

Forgetting to make her tea, Paula switched off the light and made her way up the stairs to her room.

The following morning, she approached the library with trepidation. Before opening the door, she took a deep breath, then turned the handle. Once inside, she stood under the painting and found the figure, standing on the bank, clutching the reeds. No dagger.

Tiredness can make you hallucinate, and it was very late. Just one of those things.

Time to put this nonsense out of her head and get on with her research. She went over to the desk and switched on her laptop. An hour later, she had whittled the care homes down to a manageable handful. She eliminated many of them because they had only opened in the last thirty-eight years. She then sent off emails enquiring if any of them had records of a former resident called Adeline Ogilvy.

She had sent off four when an alert told her an email had arrived in her inbox.

Lakeside Care Home had consulted their archives and had indeed had a resident by that name at that time. They were more helpful than she could have hoped for, asking her to supply them with details of what she wished to know and why.

Immediately, Paula dashed off an email to the manager, Natalie Broadhurst, asking if she had any information on what had happened to Adeline Ogilvy in her final days.

Two hours later, the reply pinged into her inbox.

> *Dear Mrs. Bancroft. The information I have is a little sketchy, I'm afraid. Mrs. Ogilvy's principal Care Assistant, Jennifer Hollingale, supplied most of it and it is not up to the standard of reporting we would expect today, nor are we able to communicate with Miss Hollingale as she died a few years ago. Briefly, she stated that Mrs. Ogilvy had suffered a severe stroke, which robbed her of speech and paralyzed her limbs, except for her left arm. She had no living relatives and had outlived her friends and acquaintances, so she rarely had visitors. Three weeks after her hundredth birthday, a woman calling herself Gerda Zimic asked to see her. Jennifer reported that there was something "a little odd" about the woman. Her English was impeccable, although she*

introduced herself as Austrian—the new owner of a house Mrs. Ogilvy had worked in many years before. Fräulein Zimic had come to pay her respects to the lady on reaching such a great age. Despite her reservations, Jennifer thought it would boost Mrs. Ogilvy's morale to have a visitor, so she took her to the old lady's room. Jennifer then left the two alone for ten minutes or so. When she returned, the woman had gone and Mrs. Ogilvy had passed away. Jennifer then becomes somewhat hysterical in her report, referring to the old lady's "wide, staring eyes" and her left hand, which was still clutching the bedsheets. The postmortem revealed that Mrs. Ogilvy died from a massive cardiac arrest, so at least she was spared any further suffering. I hope this helps with your enquiries. If I can help in any other way, please let me know.

Gerda Zimic. Unusual name. Google returned no results for it. Paula had reached a dead end, but at least she now knew that when Anna had told her of Adeline Ogilvy being frightened to death, there was some basis in truth. So how accurate were the other stories?

Paula closed her laptop and wandered over to the comfortable chair that had become hers. She picked up the book from the small table, and it slipped out of her hand, landing with a soft thud on the rug. A piece of yellowing paper fluttered out of it.

A letter. On London University's letterhead notepaper.

My dear Adeline,

I am most intrigued by your letter—so intrigued in fact, that I dropped all my commitments and headed posthaste for Vienna, where I am staying at the Hotel König von Ungarn, near the cathedral. I shall be pleased if you would join me for coffee there on Saturday of this week at 10:30 in the morning.

It was signed *Jakob Mayer, Prof.* So, what had intrigued a professor so much that he had dropped everything and traveled to Vienna on the strength of a secretary's letter? Clearly the two knew each other, but even still…

Googling Professor Mayer brought far more results. Over the next half hour, Paula learned he had been Professor of Ancient History at the university and had died in a train wreck between Vienna and Trieste in 1913. He was the author of many learned works on ancient Egypt, and much else besides. There was no mention of any association with Emeryk Quintillus, and Paula knew it was fruitless to Google *him*, as her last search had revealed nothing. Not even one mention on the entire Internet that she could trace. It was as if the man had never existed or had ensured all trace of him had been expunged from any public record.

Searching for Adeline Ogilvy turned up a similar blank, but at least that was understandable. She hadn't been noted for anything in particular. On a whim, Paula searched for Markus von Dürnstein. Various results came up, referring to his role in the family, his business interests, and contacts with many of the world's leading political figures from the 1950s through to the 1970s. She clicked on "images" and a few black-and-white photographs emerged. Color photographs of a family wedding also popped up. By the poses and family resemblance, it looked as if Markus's daughter, or at least a close relation, had been the bride.

On the outside of the smiling group, a little old lady stood out for her apparent Britishness. Her white hair was topped with a navy hat and she wore a simple, well-tailored matching suit, with an ankle-length hemline. Paula could imagine her own grandmother looking much like her. With a sudden rush of excitement, she wondered. Could this be Adeline Ogilvy? But what would she be doing in a von Dürnstein wedding photograph?

The more Paula researched, the more drawn in she became. She was about to move on when she realized she had alighted on a site dedicated to photographs featuring unexplained ghostly figures. Peering more closely, she searched the photograph for anything strange. The background appeared to be a luxury hotel. The formally posed picture showed a happy, smiling bride and groom flanked by their nearest and dearest, but, faintly, right behind the old lady, Paula could make out a barely discernible figure. Too indistinct for any distinguishing features, but female, with long hair.

She read the caption underneath.

The von Dürnstein and von Auersberg families were surprised to find the ghostly shape standing over their guest's shoulder in this wedding photo taken in 1965. It is believed that Count Markus von Dürnstein (pictured next to his niece, Sophia) may have had an idea as to the identity of the apparition. Despite many tests, the authenticity of this photograph has never been disproved and the ghostly presence remains a mystery.

Paula copied and saved the image. Further searches failed to deliver any significant information and, finally, she closed her laptop and wandered into the kitchen. Coffee beckoned. Once again, her eyes were drawn to the basement door. She stared at it, wondering what lay beyond. No smell of lilies today, thankfully.

She sipped her coffee. When the phone rang, she jumped.

The familiar voice was a welcome one. "Hi, Paula. It's Dee. How are you settling in?"

Paula's kid sister. Not a kid anymore, but a thirty-eight-year-old divorced mother of grown-up twins.

"Dee, it's so good to hear from you. We're fine. I'm on my own here for a few weeks. Phil had to go to New York."

"And he didn't take you with him? Shame on him," Dee laughed.

"I've only just arrived here. Besides, it gives me a chance to sort things out and make the place our own." Well, that had been the intention anyway. Not that she had accomplished much toward that so far. All her ideas on improving the décor, choosing and buying pictures, a few bright cushions and rugs, had all been shelved. "I'm attempting to learn German and I've done a fair bit of sketching, so it isn't all lazing around in the sunshine. Anyway, tell me all your news. How are the kids doing at university?"

While Dee chattered away, Paula became more and more fixated on the basement door. It seemed to undulate like a small wave. She rubbed her eyes with her free hand and looked again. Nothing. But when it happened again, she gave a little gasp.

"Paula, are you okay?"

"Yes…I…something weird's going on."

"Like what?"

How could she tell Dee—practical, down-to-earth Dee—that a solid door was…melting in front of her eyes?

"I…don't know how to describe it, but…" Oh, what the hell. Let her scoff! "It's the latest in a string of peculiar things that have been happening since we arrived. I thought it had stopped but… I think this house may be haunted."

There was silence on the other end of the phone followed by a loud burst of laughter. "Haunted? Are you serious? I think being on your own is turning you stir-crazy."

Paula winced. "If you could see what I'm looking at right now, you might change your mind." Paula backed farther away from the door. More silence on the other end of the phone. Dee broke it after a few seconds.

"Right, that's it. You're on. I'm due some time off work anyway. I'll check with my boss tomorrow and come over as soon as I can. Okay?"

Relief. "Thanks, Dee. I'd appreciate that."

Her sister's tone became serious. "You mean this, don't you? You actually think the place is haunted. What is it you're looking at?"

"It's stopped now, and I know this is going to sound crazy, but a few minutes ago, a heavy wooden door started to look as if it was dissolving. It didn't become transparent or anything, but it definitely didn't seem solid anymore."

Another pause. "Paula, you're not taking anything…any medication or…anything?"

"No. Dee. I'm not on any drugs, medicinal or otherwise. And it's not only the door, either." Paula told her what had happened in the room on the top floor, about the figure in the painting, the lighter, and the sketches.

Dee whistled. "Looks like I'm in for an interesting visit. Can't wait to see the house, by the way. Those photos you emailed look amazing. That library! It's not everyone that has a Klimt original painted on the ceiling in their house."

They finished their call and Paula returned to her laptop. She found the file where she had stored the photos she had taken when they first moved in. A few clicks later and she stared at the one of the library that Dee had referred to. She concentrated on the figure of the young woman on the shore; zoomed in closer to the girl's left hand. She was clutching reeds. Paula moistened her dry lips and stood. She moved under the painting and took a deep breath.

There stood the girl—her hand clutching…a gleaming dagger. Paula stumbled back and grabbed hold of a chair to steady herself. She snatched up her phone and quickly snapped the painting. Hardly daring to take her eyes off the ceiling, she swiped the camera to show the photograph she had just snapped. The girl's hand…impossibly clutching reeds. Paula glanced up at the painting and back down at the photograph. Again and again she looked back and forth. Each time, the same detail differed. Paula let her attention move to the charismatic figure of the great queen, who stared down at her through eyes that seemed all too real.

She caught her breath. Movement out in the hall.

She opened the door a crack and breathed a sigh of relief. Anna.

"Good morning, Paula. How are you today?"

"Better now," she said and waved away Anna's inquisitive look. "It's nothing. I've been having a confusing morning. Could I ask you to pop in here for a moment?"

Anna nodded and followed her into the library. Paula pointed up at the painting.

"Have a look at the girl on the riverbank. Do you see what she's holding?"

"It looks like…maybe…I'm not sure what you call them in English. In Italian we call them *canne*. They grow in the water. Here, they are in her way, so she has taken hold of them."

"Reeds," Paula said in a whisper.

"I'm not sure I understand why you asked me this question?"

Paula forced a smile. "It's nothing, honestly. Don't let me hold you up. I know you're giving the kitchen a good scrub today and I really appreciate it."

Anna left, a quizzical expression on her face. Paula left the library, sketch pad in hand. An afternoon spent sketching the Grecian-style Parliament building would take her mind off the increasing craziness in this house.

Dee called Paula at around six that evening. "I'm flying out in two days. Do you think you can stay out of mischief until then?"

"Cheeky. I'll pick you up at the airport."

"Great. I'm flying British Airways and the plane is due to arrive at four p.m."

She had just hung up when a familiar ring announced an incoming Skype call. Phil's smiling face greeted her.

"Hi, honey."

"Hi, honey yourself. Gone all American on me now, have you?"

"It's infectious. You're looking happier than when I last spoke to you. I was a bit worried. No more spooky goings-on?"

Paula sidestepped his question. "I just got off the phone with Dee. She's coming over for a few days, the day after tomorrow."

Phil grimaced.

"It's ages since I spent any quality time with my sister, and this way I won't have to endure hours of the two of you sparring and trying to score points off each other."

"I expect she has as much love for me as I do for her."

"I suspect you're right. Anyway, you're looking less exhausted, thank goodness."

"Yes, well it's only lunchtime here. I'll be in the office for at least another six hours…probably longer. I keep finding more and more problems. I can't talk about them on an unsecured line, but you wouldn't believe the mess the place has been left in."

"You'll sort it out. That's what they pay you for. Troubleshooter extraordinaire."

"Been getting on with your sketching? You won't get much done when Denise the Menace arrives."

"Don't call her that. You know she hates it."

"Good job she can't hear me then."

"I think we'd better not Skype when she's here. I can't trust you not to say something that would upset her. We'll just use our phones instead."

"If she can't take a joke at her age… Damn. I'm sorry, love, I have to go, someone's calling me. I'll ring you tomorrow."

"Love you."

"Me too."

Paula put her phone in her jeans pocket and glanced up at the painting. The figure was once again holding reeds. A chill cloaked her, and she shivered, even though it felt too warm for a fire.

Above her, the timbers creaked. *An old house. It happens.*

But what about that scratching in the wall?

Like the sound of scurrying claws, the noise moved along one wall and down another. Paula forced herself to get closer to the source of the sound. She put her ear against the wall and, steadying herself with her hands, palms flat, she moved along, following the scratching. It stopped. She stayed pressed against the wall for some moments, but no more sounds emerged.

She tried to work out where the cause of the noise could be located. One of the walls was an exterior, but not the one where the sound had come from. Another wall separated the library from the hall and the dining room lay on the other side of the last wall.

Paula went outside and edged her way along the corridor to the dining room door. Inside, she hurried to the dividing wall and listened. Silence. No scurrying. She stepped back. Something didn't quite add up. She hurried into the kitchen, opened a drawer and pulled out a tape measure. A few minutes later, she had completed her calculations. Sure enough, she had found a discrepancy. It appeared the walls must be a good six feet thick. Six feet of solid bricks and mortar. So how would there be any room for any rodent to get in there? Unless, of course, it wasn't all solid wall. Perhaps a hollow existed between the two rooms. Maybe a narrow passageway.

Tomorrow, she would ring the estate agent. If there *was* an infestation, something would have to be done about it.

Paula had drifted off to sleep on a cloudy and moonless night when she shot awake. She lay in the dark, listening for any sound. Hearing none, she started to settle back down again.

And stopped.

This time, there could be no mistaking it. More scurrying. Coming from the wall behind her. In an instant, Paula leaped out of bed and craned her neck, pressing her ear as hard as she could against the wall. Was she imagining a…sort of…whispering? Faint, then fainter. Now it had stopped altogether. No more scratching. But there had been something there, of that she was certain. Something that shouldn't be there. Hopefully only mice. The thought it might be some unknown, unseen manifestation of her nightmares was one she fought hard to suppress. No, it had to be mice. Or rats. She shuddered.

Paula rose at five, feeling exhausted. She'd had no more sleep. Downstairs, she drank two cups of strong coffee and forced herself to eat toast. Finally, at nine a.m., she rang Stefan.

"I can assure you, no one has ever reported an infestation of any kind before, Mrs. Bancroft."

She fought to control the anger building up inside her. He thought she had made it up. Some sort of silly, hysterical woman. She wouldn't stand for that. Her lip curled as she barely controlled her anger. "And *I* can assure *you* that I know what I heard. You need to either get a pest-control company out here or inform the family so they can make arrangements."

As usual, Stefan responded by pouring liberal quantities of oil over his voice. "I am sure there is no need to trouble the family over this, Mrs. Bancroft. I will arrange for someone to come out to you today." He hung up before Paula could berate him for his attitude.

"Patronizing, arrogant bastard," she said into the dead phone, and exhaled loudly.

Three hours later, a short man with jet-black hair, bushy eyebrows and a high-visibility jacket arrived with a white van and a selection of tools. He spoke little English but had obviously been briefed. By gestures and Paula's limited German, she succeeded in communicating where she had detected the problems. She left him to his work and made them both coffee.

Around half an hour later, he came back. By his expression, it had not gone well, and by the stilted conversation and body language that followed, it seemed he had found no trace of any pests, or any way they could have got in. He went to the basement door and rattled it. Then he pointed to the locks. Paula shook her head and shrugged. The message had been clear, though. If she wanted to be sure the house was rodent-free, he would need to gain access to the basement. He left his card, smiled, and departed soon after.

Paula grabbed her phone and tapped Stefan's number. He answered almost immediately, but was his usual evasive self and Paula felt in no mood for his excuses.

"Stefan, this is no longer a matter of choice. If there are rats here, the pest-control man needs to get into the basement because that's the only place they could have got in. He's checked thoroughly." At least, she assumed he had.

She did not imagine the loud sigh on the other end of the phone. "Very well, Mrs. Bancroft, I will call the family, but I do not imagine they will be too pleased."

"And I am not exactly pleased to be living in a home infested with rats."

"We do not know if that is the case."

"Well, something is scratching around in the walls. Do you have another suggestion?"

"If you say so, Mrs. Bancroft, then I must believe you."

Paula picked up a nearby pencil in her right hand and snapped it clean in half. If she carried on this conversation much longer, she knew she would say something she might regret.

"Just see to it, Stefan." She cut the call.

Paula had another disturbed night. Not noises in the walls this time, but dreams of the image that had appeared in her old sketchbook. She couldn't see him clearly, but she knew he was staring at her. Waiting. He touched her and his fingers pierced her flesh like icicles.

She woke in a cold sweat, her heart beating a tattoo.

The heavy curtains rendered the bedroom almost pitch black. Only the faintest ray of amber from the streetlights outside penetrated the tiny space between them.

Paula stared out into the gloom, too scared to move. The room had taken on a strange, menacing atmosphere. Heavy, cloying. On the far wall, a pinprick of light flickered and grew rapidly into a pulsating glow. She lay, paralyzed, not trusting what she saw. The gleam intensified, became a ball of blue-white light against the gray walls. It throbbed in a bass drumbeat—building to a thumping crescendo. Paula wrenched her hands free from their paralysis and clapped them against her ears.

The ball of light shifted, changed shape, became fluid, morphing like the colors in a lava lamp. It shifted away from the wall. Came toward her. She screamed and clamped her eyes shut.

The throbbing took over her mind. Like a migraine, hammering incessantly in her temples. She no longer knew if she was asleep or awake. She curled her unwilling body into a fetal position, her breathing shallow.

It stopped.

She waited. Opened one eye. Then the other. The ball of light had gone, as if it had never existed.

But in the room a strong smell of lilies wafted toward her.

Chapter 4

"Oh my God, Paula, this is amazing." Dee set down her suitcase and stared around the hallway. "I guessed it was big, but I never imagined palatial. Posh area, too."

"I know. Hietzing is about as upmarket as you can get in Vienna, and that means pretty upmarket."

"I want to see everything while I'm here."

"That'll be tough. There's around a hundred and forty museums, for a start."

"Okay, maybe not *everything*, but I've been on the Internet and the Museum of Modern Art looks fantastic. Have you been yet?"

Paula shook her head. "We can go there and visit the other art galleries and museums in the Museumsquartier."

"I must go to the Schönbrunn Palace, as it's so near, and the Hofburg, the Spanish Riding School—"

Paula laughed. "How long are you staying?"

"Four days. Long weekend, really."

"We'll try and cram as much as we can in, but you'll have to come for another visit."

"Is Phil away for long then?"

"That is a wicked grin, Dee. Three weeks. You two have got to find a way of getting along together. Honestly, it's crazy. Two intelligent, lovely people at each other's throats within five minutes of being in the same room together."

"What can I say? He winds me up."

"Well, wind yourself down and come and look at the library."

Paula opened the door and Dee inhaled sharply.

"Wow! I knew from the photos it was amazing, but seeing it for real…" She crossed the threshold, never taking her eyes off the magnificent painting. "Those eyes… They follow you. How did he do that? It looks so alive."

"It's been restored a couple of times over the years, and they've obviously made an excellent job of it. You can tell Gustav Klimt loved women and loved painting them. His attention to detail is quite something, isn't it?"

"So, this is Cleopatra's arrival at Tarsus?"

"Yes. The legend goes that she arrived in triumph on a golden barge in order to impress, and eventually seduce, Mark Antony. Her plan worked."

Dee shivered. "Is there a window open somewhere? I just got this chilly draft down my right side."

"I don't think so." Paula checked the windows on the far wall. "No, all closed."

Dee rubbed her right arm. "Didn't you feel it? Gave me goosebumps."

Paula shook her head.

"Never mind, it's gone now." She returned her attention to the painting. "Who's the girl on the riverbank?"

"Not sure."

"Looks like she's up to no good. She's got a dagger in her hand."

Paula jumped. "You can see it, too?"

"Sorry?"

"Everyone else sees her clutching a clump of reeds. When I photographed it, the picture showed reeds. Sometimes *I* see it that way, but most of the time—like now—I see the dagger. That's when I think it must be Arsinoe, Cleopatra's sister, who stole her throne briefly and plotted to kill her. Cleopatra got in first and had her banished and then murdered."

"What a loving family."

"Oh, they were all at it in those days." Paula laughed. It made her feel better knowing she wasn't the only one who saw the dagger.

Maybe they saw the same thing because she and Dee were so closely related.

"Well, I don't know about you, but I'm starving."

"Right, I'll show you your room and you can get unpacked. Then let's take the U-bahn into the city and go for a meal."

"The Café Central. I've got to go there. Sigmund Freud used to drink coffee there…and Trotsky, Lenin. They even say the Russian Revolution was plotted there."

"We'll go tomorrow. For today, though, let's go for a pizza. I know just the place."

"Can't wait."

———

The next day, after a morning steeping themselves in Austrian Imperial history at the Hofburg, Paula sank down gratefully into a comfortable chair. The timeless elegance of the Café Central suited her mood perfectly.

Dee picked up the impressive menu and used it to shield her lips while she whispered to Paula. "The waiters are a bit fierce, aren't they?"

"They're okay once you get used to them. I've been here a few times now. I think it's because they're so proud to work here. Anyway, I'm having a Wiener mélange and some strudel. It's delicious."

"Mélange." Dee found it on the menu. "Espresso with frothed milk. That'll do me, too. I've been looking forward to my first authentic apple strudel ever since you suggested it yesterday."

As she did whenever she came here, Paula took in the opulent marble columns, the vaulted ceilings, and the central vitrine displaying more fine patisserie than she could imagine, all laid out in mouthwatering splendor. Sitting here, watching the world go by, the disturbing dreams and anomalies of life at the Villa Dürnstein seemed unreal.

The strudel arrived. Light, flaky, and perfectly spiced. Dee rolled her eyes as she took another mouthful. "I could get used to this. Not that my waistline would forgive me."

They were finishing their coffee when a man approached them.

He stopped no more than a foot away and pointed a shaking finger at Paula. He spoke so rapidly, she couldn't keep up with his German.

"What does he want?" Dee asked.

"I don't know. Something about...no, that wouldn't make any sense."

A waiter hurried up to him and, with an apologetic glance to Paula and Dee, steered the man away and out of the door. A few customers watched with interest and then resumed their conversations.

The waiter returned. "I am so sorry that man disturbed you," he said, in perfect English.

"Who is he?" Paula asked.

"I don't know. He isn't one of our regular customers. I think he is...not well." He tapped his head.

"Did you hear what he said to us?" Dee asked. "He sounded quite angry."

"He said a *Geist*...I don't know the word in English. A person who is dead but comes back."

"A ghost?" Paula said.

"Ah, ghost. Yes. He said a ghost was standing behind you."

"A *ghost*?" Dee exclaimed.

"Yes." The waiter looked uncomfortable, as if he wondered whether he should have told them.

"And that was it?" Paula said. "All that gesticulating, finger-pointing... Did he say anything else, or describe it?"

The waiter shifted uncomfortably. "No, Madame. That is all." He left before Paula could prod him any further.

"He didn't tell us everything," Dee said.

"Clearly. But why?"

"Didn't want to frighten us. The man was obviously deranged. A bit weird, though. Is this place supposed to be haunted, then?"

"Oh, I expect so. It's pretty old. It used to be a palace. Like practically every other building in central Vienna."

"I'm certainly getting my money's worth on this trip," Dee said. "I've only been here a day and I've already managed to upset the locals."

Paula laughed. "Only one local. Come on. I'll pay and then let's get back home." She felt glad she could make light of it for Dee's sake, but the incident had upset her more than she cared to admit. She couldn't be certain, but she thought she had heard the man use the word "*Teufel.*" The more she replayed the scene in her mind, the more sure she became. The waiter had lied. The man hadn't said there was a ghost behind her, he had said the devil stood there. Paula shivered. Goosebumps raised on her arms.

Back home, Paula and Dee sank into the well-upholstered chairs in the living room. Paula's feet throbbed freely as she removed shoes that had grown too tight.

Dee sighed. "I loved the Hofburg. Even if it was a little hard on the feet. And that strudel…" She raised her eyes heavenward. "To die for. Pity about the weirdo, though."

Paula changed the subject. "I don't know about you, but I need a leisurely soak in a hot, scented bath, with plenty of bubbles."

Dee leaned back. "Sounds like heaven."

Paula dragged herself up on her protesting feet and picked up her shoes. "Help yourself to anything you want. I'll see you later." But Dee had already dozed off.

Paula lay back in the welcoming warmth of the orange-scented bubbles and closed her eyes. The throbbing in her feet had subsided, and she was in danger of falling asleep. She opened her eyes again and immersed herself up to her chin.

She jumped at a sudden noise from outside the bathroom. Dee must have woken and come upstairs to her room next door. Paula waited for the sound of the taps being turned on. Outside, in her bedroom, the floorboards creaked.

She called out. "Dee?"

No reply.

The floorboards creaked again. "Dee? Did you want something?"

No reply.

The door handle slowly turned. Paula stood and grabbed a large towel. She wrapped it around herself, never taking her eyes off the handle. It barely moved at all. Then it stopped. Paula waited a few seconds, summoning up the courage to investigate. She chided herself for being scared. It could only be Dee. Probably trying to scare her on purpose. Paula took a deep breath and wrenched the door open. "Dee?"

She crossed the floor, out of the bedroom, into the next bathroom. No trace of Dee. She opened the door of the guest room. Still no sign of her sister.

Perplexed, she turned and wandered back to her room.

In the bathroom, she wiped the fogged mirror and removed the clips she had used to secure her hair. She shook her head.

In the mirror, a face stared back at her. *That* face.

Paula screamed.

It vanished.

But it had been there. The face she had seen in her nightmares. In the sketch pad. Bearded, hollow-eyed. Real.

Paula daren't move. She lost track of how long she stood there.

When she finally emerged from her room, fully dressed, Dee had just reached the top of the stairs. Clearly, her sister hadn't heard her scream, and Paula wouldn't worry her by telling her what she thought she had seen. She pasted a smile on her face. "Had a good sleep?" she asked, relieved that her voice sounded calm.

Dee yawned. "I must have dropped off as soon as I sat down. We certainly walked a few miles today. Enjoy your bath?"

"Mostly. Did you come up earlier?"

"No. I've only just woken up. Going to grab a quick shower."

She disappeared into her room and Paula descended the staircase, still trying to work out what she had seen in that mirror. She couldn't help wondering if the man in the Café Central had seen the same apparition. But that would mean it could transport itself out of the house. It could follow her. Anywhere.

She had reached the kitchen door when she heard Dee's scream.

She raced up the stairs to find her sister sitting on the bed, trembling and white-faced.

Paula put her arms around her and held her close. "Whatever's happened?"

Dee struggled to speak through chattering teeth. "I saw…a man." She shook her head. "Not a man… Someone… Something.

I…it…he…had black eyes. No…it had…no eyes. Its face was gray…with a black beard. It stared at me."

Paula's heart sank like a stone. "Hush, Dee, you're okay. I'm here. There's something I need to tell you."

"What?"

Paula took a deep breath. "I've seen it, too."

"What is it? *Who* is it?"

"I don't know. I wish I did."

"So, that's what you meant when you said you thought this house is haunted. I should have believed you."

"Why should you? You have to experience it before you can truly believe."

"You've got to get rid of it. Exorcism or something."

"I wouldn't have a clue where to begin with something like that. I'll have to wait until Phil gets back. He's the one who speaks fluent German. He's also the Catholic in the family. Nominally, anyway."

"But he's not back for over two weeks. You can't stay here with…that."

Paula did her best to sound nonchalant. "How bad can it be? It's not as if it's done anything. It only looked at us."

"That's quite enough for me. You were always the brave one. Even when we were children, I always came to you when I got scared." Dee's chattering told Paula how scared she really felt. "And do you remember that new girl in your year at school? Sally? Poor kid was being terrorized by that bully. Melanie."

Paula thought for a moment and then the memory of it flooded back.

Dee laughed nervously. "Everyone else was too scared of her to do anything, but you waded in there and hauled her off. That dreadful bully might have been twice your size but that didn't stop you from smacking her across the face. That taught her."

Paula smiled. "She never bullied Sally again, that's for sure. She never messed with me, either—or you, for that matter."

Dee took deep breaths and gradually recovered her composure. "I think I'll have that shower," she said. "It might help calm me down."

Paula nodded. "You sure you'll be all right? I can stay if you want."

"No, I'll be fine." She didn't sound it. "Like you said. It hasn't done anything to me. Just stared. If it was even there at all."

Paula said nothing. If it helped Dee to think she had imagined it, so be it. She left her sister and went downstairs. In the dining room, she poured herself a large brandy, another one for Dee, and sat at the table. Her mind played with theory after theory until she found one that seemed to answer at least some of the questions.

Dee joined her a few minutes later, dressed, but with her hair wrapped in a towel. She accepted the drink. "Thanks, I need this." She took a deep swig and set her glass down on a coaster.

"We need to find out who he…it…is," she said, at last.

"I think I may know the answer to that," Paula said.

A loud crash echoed from the kitchen.

"What the hell?" Paula raced out of the dining room, closely followed by Dee.

At first, it seemed everything was in order. No broken glass or plates. No upturned drawers.

"Over here," Dee called. She stood in front of the basement door. "You're not going to believe this."

Paula started toward her and gasped. A massive gash ran from top to bottom of the door, as if someone had taken an ax to it. From the other side.

"What the…?" Paula stared at it.

Dee whispered, "Have you seen the padlocks?"

Paula hadn't at first, because they weren't where they should have been. Then she saw them. Side by side on the floor. Unlocked.

"I think something wants us to open that door," Dee said.

"And all of a sudden, I really don't want to."

"Looks like we don't have much of a choice."

Paula grabbed her sister's hand as, by itself, the door unlatched and started to creak open on hinges that sounded as if they hadn't been used in decades.

A smell of decay and stale air hit them.

Dee whispered, "Dear God, how can that happen?"

Paula could only stare. At a 45-degree angle, the door stopped moving.

Dee nudged Paula. "What do we do now?"

"I say we go in there, but not unarmed."

"You're kidding me, right?"

"Dee, I can't let this go. I have to find out why the count locked the basement up like this in the first place."

Dee stared at her. "Aren't you the least bit scared?"

Paula laughed. "Scared? I'm bloody terrified. Now, are you with me or not?"

"I'm certainly not letting you go in there alone. But what the fuck do you arm yourself with when your opponent isn't…tangible?"

"I have no idea, but a couple of flashlights wouldn't go amiss. If there's any electricity down there, it's probably ancient." Paula opened cupboard doors until she found what she needed. A small collection of flashlights of different sizes had been stacked on the bottom shelf. She selected the two largest and handed one to Dee. They switched the beams on.

"At least the batteries are still working," Paula said.

"For now, anyway. So what do we arm ourselves with? A rolling pin?"

"At least we'd be prepared if we ran into any rats or cockroaches or something." She grabbed a heavy marble rolling pin out of one of the drawers.

Dee laughed a little too hysterically.

"What's so funny?"

"You, brandishing that thing."

Paula rummaged through the knife drawer and drew out a vicious-looking meat cleaver. "Your choice. Pin or cleaver, which do you want?"

Dee stared disbelievingly at her sister. "You're serious, aren't you?"

"Never more so. Rolling pin or cleaver."

"I'll take the rolling pin. I could probably bash something, but I don't think I could chop it up."

Paula moistened her dry lips. "Okay, let's do this."

She pushed the door open sufficiently to let them in and switched on her flashlight. Dee followed her, and their twin beams swept around the bare, grubby walls.

"That smell…" Paula wrinkled her nose against the sickly, dank stench and breathed through her mouth. Her beam picked up an old-fashioned light switch. She turned it twice. Nothing happened. "Wires have probably corroded, or the bulb's had it," she said.

A steep staircase led down into the darkness. "This is it. Let's go." Paula grabbed the handrail and began her descent, closely followed by her sister.

At the bottom, their footsteps echoed off the walls. The smell grew stronger. A mixture of rotting vegetation and the sickly sweetness of lilies, mingled with the stench of something long dead and forgotten.

Dee whispered in Paula's ear. "I really don't like this. Let's go back."

"No, we've got to see what's down here." They shone their beams around a room. Copper pans hung on the walls, an old range took up half of one side of the kitchen, and a scrubbed pine table formed the centerpiece. "Let's keep going," Paula said.

They made their way out through an open door, along a narrow corridor, past a room that still contained a collection of dusty wine bottles on racks. Paula's flashlight picked up a closed door directly ahead. When she reached it, she turned the handle and the door opened, as if it had been used regularly.

Dee tugged her arm. "There's something very wrong here, can't you feel it?"

"Yes," Paula said. "That's why we have to do this."

Inside the room, the smell of rot almost overpowered them. Paula and Dee gagged. "God, that's disgusting," Paula said. "What the hell is this place?"

They shone their flashlights around and Dee gasped. "The walls. They're covered in blood."

Paula peered more closely. "Possibly. Maybe red paint. I think it's a bit too bright for dried blood. They're hieroglyphics, or at least they look like them."

Out of the corner of her eye, she caught a movement. An indistinct shadow flashed across the wall. Her heart thumping, she nudged Dee. "Did you see that?"

"What?"

"I don't know what it was, but I don't think we're alone."

"Oh, Paula, let's go. I'm going to throw up in a minute, I can feel it. The stench and this atmosphere…"

"I'm certain there's something down here. It may be important. If we could just get to the bottom of why that door managed to open itself… Maybe something is trying to help us."

"By scaring us half to death?"

Paula couldn't think of a suitable reply. She flashed her beam around, picking up broken furniture and other debris. "There's nothing." She shone her flashlight farther to the left, illuminating a small portrait. "Wow, look at this," she said.

Dee joined her.

Paula moved in front of the picture and shone her flashlight on the profile of the woman. "She looks like Cleopatra. Or pictures I've seen of her, anyway. The eye makeup and the black, braided hair. Different to the one upstairs, though. If anything, this one looks more alive. She shone the beam around the edge of the figure. "It's got to be another Klimt with all that gold. There should be a signature." She peered closer. "There it is. Gustav Klimt. But why would someone keep a Klimt original locked away down here?

Dee shook her head. "I don't know and, frankly, right now, I don't care. Let's get out of here."

Paula ignored her. She had spotted something else. "Looks like someone's had a fire here at some time. Look at the ashes."

The beam picked up an untidy heap of gray ash scattered across the floor under the portrait.

"Paula, please. This place is giving me the creeps. Let's go. You've seen what's down here. I need a drink."

Paula nodded. She reached up for the portrait and wrenched it off its hook.

"Whatever are you doing? That's not yours to take."

"I'm not taking it. Not *stealing* it. I'm sure the family must have forgotten it's down here. I'll take it up to the library. It'll look great in there. It's far too beautiful to hide away down here."

"I don't think you should move it."

"Why not?"

Dee shivered. "I don't know. It bothers me."

Paula laughed. "It's a *painting*, Dee. And I thought *you* were the skeptical one."

"I used to be. Not anymore. Not since I came to this house. Don't forget the painting in the library. Only *we* see the girl holding a dagger. There's something wrong there, and I get a similar feeling about this one."

"Okay, I admit I can't explain that. Yet. But this is a valuable Klimt portrait, and I would guess, given the subject matter, our old friend Emeryk Quintillus commissioned it. It deserves to hang where it can be admired. I can't stand for art of such quality to be hidden from view."

"Even if it's evil?" Dee shuddered. "Didn't you feel that?"

"Feel what?"

"When you said his name. A cold…not exactly a draft. More like extreme cold. It touched my arm. Icy cold."

Paula touched her sister's arm, surprised to find a patch so cold, it felt as if an ice pack had been applied to it.

Another shadow flitted across her line of vision. The hairs on the back of her neck prickled. Thankfully, it didn't appear Dee had seen it. Her sister was already jumpy enough for both of them.

"You're right," Paula said, keeping her voice steady. "Let's take this and go. I think we've seen all there is to see and we're still none the wiser."

Paula tucked the painting under her arm and the two of them retraced their steps back up to the kitchen. Once Dee had come through the door, Paula shut it. "Will you look at that?" She pointed to the door. "Not a mark on it now. Did we imagine that huge gash?"

Dee shook her head. "No, it was there all right."

Paula heard a click and tried the handle. "It's locked from the inside. Don't ask. I can't explain that, either."

Dee pointed to the painting, still tucked under Paula's arm. "I wish you hadn't brought that up."

"Don't be daft. Let's have a proper look at it. She laid down the flashlight and the cleaver and placed the portrait on the kitchen table. In the bright fluorescent kitchen light, the colors were revealed in all their vivid freshness.

Dee touched it and immediately withdrew her hand. "Weird texture. Not like oil paint. It's grainy, powdery even. Has any of it come off on you?"

Paula examined her sleeve. "No. It can't still be wet. Not after all these years. Maybe it's the damp down there."

"Maybe."

Paula touched the surface. Dee was right. Not a pleasant experience. Grainy, powdery and almost sticky, except that nothing actually rubbed off.

"I'll get a picture hook and hang it now. You fix us another couple of drinks."

Paula watched as Dee seemed to drag her heels to the dining room. In all the years she had known her, Paula could not remember one time Dee had been this anxious. She was normally so practical, down-to-earth, nothing fazed her. This house had really affected her.

Paula opened a drawer she knew contained various tools, nails, screws, and a small hammer. She found what she needed. A packet of picture hooks lay among the detritus that had accumulated there.

She picked up the painting, picture hook and hammer. Dee emerged with a bottle of cognac and two glasses and followed her sister into the library.

"Here, I think," Paula said.

Dee stared up at the ceiling painting. "That dagger looks brighter today," she said, her voice not much more than a whisper.

Paula paused in the act of hammering in the picture hook and joined her.

"Surely her hand wasn't raised like that?" Paula wished she hadn't spoken her thoughts out loud. Dee would be bound to be even more unnerved.

"She looks like she's ready to strike. To kill someone. Cleopatra maybe." She stepped back and looked away. "Paula, this house...it's not right."

"I think we're letting our imaginations run riot."

"Oh? Just how much of this has been our imagination and how much actually happened? The gashed door? The open padlocks? The stench? *This...*" She jabbed her finger up at the painting. "You say everyone else sees her clutching at reeds. Photographs show her clutching at reeds, even when we're staring at that fucking dagger."

Her voice grew higher until hysteria set in. Tears streamed down Dee's face. Shocked, Paula lay down the hammer and rushed to comfort her. "Come on, sit down, have some more brandy." Dee allowed herself to be steered toward an armchair. She sat on the edge and Paula placed a glass, lavishly charged with Courvoisier, into her trembling hands. She guided it up to her sister's lips and Dee took a large gulp, coughing as it burned her throat. She took another sip and gradually the trembling ceased.

"Sorry," she said. "I don't know what came over me."

"Don't apologize. It's everything that's been happening."

"I don't know how you can remain so calm."

"I'm not, but I'm your big sister, aren't I? Not allowed to fall apart."

Dee managed a wobbly smile. It left her face almost as soon as it had arrived. "You're not going to stay here, are you? I mean, when Phil gets back. Before, maybe. You'll find somewhere else to live? Somewhere…safer?"

Paula hammered the picture hook in and picked up the painting before replying. "That's not so easy, I'm afraid. We signed a three-year lease."

"Surely you could get out of it in the circumstances."

"What circumstances? I can see the look on that smarmy estate agent's face when I tell him, 'Sorry Stefan, the place is haunted, we have to leave and terminate our lease forthwith.' He's going to love that."

"But this house…"

Paula positioned the portrait on its new hook and stepped back. "There. That looks gorgeous."

"Gives me the creeps. Her expression."

"You can only see half of it. She's in profile."

"Even so. It doesn't take a great deal of imagination to picture the rest of her face."

"Maybe you should take up painting, too." Paula changed the subject. "Tomorrow let's go round the Schönbrunn Palace. I've heard it's amazing."

Dee nodded, slowly. "Anything to get out of this house." She held out her glass and Paula poured more brandy.

"That figure I saw," Dee said.

"Yes?"

"I'm sure he's at the heart of this. We're slap-bang in the middle of something that's as much a part of this house as the bricks and mortar."

"Maybe."

"It's got to be Quintillus, hasn't it? Oh God, there it is again." She rubbed her arm.

"What?"

"Like cold fingers gripping my arm."

"I don't feel anything."

"It's the same feeling I got in the basement. And *you'd* just said his name then."

Paula touched Dee's arm, but unlike earlier, it felt warm. Normal. She shook her head.

"Look, I'm *telling* you. Something just grabbed my arm."

"I don't disbelieve you, Dee. Honestly I don't. Some crazy stuff is happening."

"We need to find out more about him."

"Don't think I haven't tried. There's total Internet silence on him. It's as if he never existed."

"But *we* know he did. We know he worked at Oxford University, and we know approximately when. They're bound to have records."

"We only know through hearsay and local legend but, yes, it's not a bad place to start. Not tonight though, please. It's been quite a day. Tomorrow, before we go out, I'll find an email address."

A thump sounded from the upper level of the library. Dee and Paula jumped.

"What the hell was that?" Dee asked.

Paula raced over to the spiral staircase. She made her way carefully up it. Once at the top, she saw a large leather-bound volume lying haphazardly on the walkway. She made her way toward it and bent to pick up the book, which had fallen open on a new chapter heading—"Arsinoe." Keeping her finger in the page, Paula turned it so that the spine faced her.

Dee called from below. "What is it?"

"*Lives of the Ptolemies*, by Professor Jakob Mayer. That's the same name as on that note I showed you. The one addressed to Adeline." Paula brought the book downstairs. She showed Dee where it had fallen open.

"She keeps turning up, doesn't she?" Paula said.

Dee made a harrumphing noise. "Are you going to tell me it was just coincidence that this book should fall off the shelf at that moment?"

Paula didn't reply. She had turned to the frontispiece. "Professor Jakob Mayer was at the University of London. This book was published in 1903, and if the local gossip has any basis in truth, this makes him a contemporary of…" Paula didn't say his name. It clearly affected Dee. "Our friend."

"He'd be long dead now, though."

Paula nodded. "But maybe there's a link there somewhere. I'll mention him in my email. Perhaps they knew of him at Oxford."

Dee yawned. "Sorry, I think it's the brandy. I can't keep my eyes open. Can I bunk down with you tonight? I'd rather not be on my own in that room after what happened."

" 'Course you can. It'll be like old times."

Dee smiled. Paula wished she didn't look so pale. A pang of remorse hit her. Why had she asked her to come and stay? But then, Dee had basically invited herself. She had always been a law unto herself, and even if Paula had tried to dissuade her, she'd probably have come anyway.

Dee stood, yawned again and picked up her glass. Paula laid the book down on the coffee table and drained her brandy. She followed Dee out to the kitchen where her sister rinsed their glasses in the sink.

Paula switched off the kitchen light. "Damn, I forgot. I've left the book I'm reading in the library. I'll see you upstairs in a minute."

Dee started up the stairs and Paula hurried into the library. She went to switch on the light and stopped short.

A greenish glow pulsated around the ceiling, illuminating the girl on the riverbank. Paula shut her eyes, pressed the switch and flooded the room with light. When she opened her eyes, the greenish glow had gone.

Her heart thumped painfully as she retrieved her latest book, *The War of the Worlds*, and avoided staring at the painting. A movement out of the corner of her eye made her glance at the portrait. The gold shimmered. As Paula watched, she could swear a tiny spark lit up the one visible eye of the portrait's subject. Paula snapped the light off, closed the door firmly and, with trembling hands, mounted the stairs.

Dee greeted her in the bedroom where she had changed into pajamas. One look at her sister's face was enough. "What's happened now?"

Before Paula could stop herself, she blurted it out.

"The portrait. I think it's alive."

Chapter 5

Dee turned around from the portrait as Paula entered the library. "Good morning," Dee said, smiling. "You slept well."

Paula ignored the inaccuracy of that statement. She had taken hours to get to sleep, jumping at every slight noise. It must have been after five when she finally dropped off. "You got up bright and early and I didn't even notice."

"I woke at seven and you were sleeping so peacefully, I didn't want to disturb you."

"How are you feeling today?"

"Much better." Dee stretched. "It's funny how daylight puts everything into perspective, isn't it? This, for example." She pointed at the portrait. "In artificial light, we read all sorts of sinister things into it and now, in the light of the spring sunshine, we can see it for what it is. An exquisite example of a great artist's work. It isn't alive. It can't stare back at us, and you were right when you said it shouldn't be hidden."

Paula had fully intended to take it off the wall, shove it in a drawer, and attempt to forget about it, but as she approached it, she saw what Dee meant. Sunshine flooded the library and bathed the portrait in golden light. Paula took in the subject's regal posture, the slightly hooked nose and that brilliant, charismatic eye. Granted, it brimmed with life, but it was a painting. How could she have been so scared? Paula shook her head.

"You're right, Dee. We wound each other up quite a bit last night. There's enough weirdness going on here without creating any more." Paula stared hard at her sister. She seemed different, somehow.

"You're looking quite radiant today. I was worried; you were so pale yesterday."

Dee smiled. Her eyes lit up. "Makeup. I didn't wear any yesterday."

"Suits you." But Paula remained unconvinced. "You're not pregnant, are you?"

"Good God, no! Roger's had the snip anyway. Remember, I told you? Last year."

Paula did remember. "You have a glow about you, that's all."

"Do I? Well, I'm definitely not pregnant. It's the makeup. Anyway, when are we going to the Palace?"

"I thought around eleven."

"You know, it's weird, but I really do feel much better today. I'm not jumping at shadows anymore."

"Glad to hear it. Ready for some more history, then?"

Dee nodded. "Bring it on."

She seemed so rejuvenated and animated. In contrast, Paula felt tired and in need of a good night's sleep not punctuated by recurring nightmares and strange apparitions.

At the Schönbrunn Palace, they passed through room after sumptuous room, marveling at the enormous crystal chandeliers, the ornate mirrors and sheer opulence. The beautiful face of the tragic Empress Elisabeth surveyed them from portraits and photographs. Her eyes held a haunted quality.

"It's as if she's begging to be freed from her lavish prison," Paula said, not realizing she had spoken out loud.

"Bit dramatic," Dee said. "Anyway, what had she got to complain about? No money problems for her, no worrying where her next meal was coming from."

"I doubt she would have been too bothered about that. She barely ate anything, and she obsessed about her weight," Paula said. "But she was terribly unhappy. She had no freedom. Certainly not when she lived here, anyway. She went abroad a lot, but tragedy seemed to follow her wherever she went. Her son committed suicide after killing his mistress, and she herself was assassinated in Switzerland. The emperor never got over it."

"Thank you for the history lesson."

Dee had positively snapped at her.

"What's the matter?" Paula asked, linking her arm through her sister's. All the earlier enthusiasm had drained from Dee's face.

Dee gently freed herself from her sister's grasp. "Just ignore me. I felt fine this morning but for some reason, I'm in a way with myself again."

Paula gave a half smile at the odd turn of phrase. Their mother had used that expression to describe herself, or someone she knew, when they were down or depressed.

"I suppose it's all the stuff that's been going on in that house," Paula said. "I'll have a word with Phil tonight when he rings me. I think the time has come to seriously consider whether we can stay there—lease or no lease."

They moved to one side to let a party of excited young Japanese tourists pass. Dee's eyes locked onto Paula's. "I've been thinking about that. I don't think you should move out. Not yet anyway."

That was unexpected. "Eh? Last night you were all for getting out there and then."

"I know, but as I said this morning, in the daylight, you see things in perspective. Maybe the place is haunted. Maybe it isn't. You know me, until now, I've always had a tough time believing anything like that anyway. In the dark, an old house, creaks, tricks of the light—"

"Come on, Dee, you know it's a lot more than that. That basement door—"

"Okay, maybe I'm oversimplifying a bit—"

"A *bit*?"

"All right then. A lot. As you said, though, you've signed a three-year lease and the landlord isn't going to release you from it simply because you think the place is haunted."

"More's the pity."

"You've made huge changes to your life merely by coming here. Don't you owe it to yourself, and Phil, to try and stick with it? You've said yourself, he's got a lot of pressure on him right now and, to cap it all, he's thousands of miles away. He's bound to worry about you."

Paula thought for a moment. "If I move to a hotel until he comes back, he needn't know."

"And what good is that going to do? You've still got to come back."

"At least I wouldn't be alone. You've got to go back to England tomorrow."

"No, I don't. Before you got up this morning, I rang my boss. I told him you were having some problems and I needed to stay longer. He's allowed me to take a last-minute holiday. As long as I keep in touch, I've got up to two weeks. Someone will call me if anything urgent comes up."

"Understanding boss."

"It cuts both ways. He needed a lot of time off last year when his wife had a nervous breakdown. I covered for him. Now it's payback time."

Paula wasn't sure she liked the way Dee said that. It sounded mean somehow after what her boss had just agreed to. She pushed the thought aside. Dee had made a generous gesture. "You've certainly had a change of heart, but I can't say I won't appreciate your company. I really don't think I could stay in that house on my own anymore."

"It'll be fine, you'll see. Perfectly fine."

They carried on with their tour, stepping into the lavishly paneled Walnut Room. The party of Japanese were chattering excitedly. A few of them smiled at Dee and Paula, who smiled back. Suddenly, one girl screamed. She pointed at Dee, her hand shaking.

"What is it? What's wrong?" Dee turned every which way to see what could have caused the girl to cry out. She had started to sob hysterically and had to be comforted by her friends. An older, male member of the party came up to Paula and Dee.

"Excuse me. I am sorry but she says she saw something. Standing behind you," he indicated Dee. "A woman, but not a real woman. A ghost woman."

"Can she describe her?"

The man nodded. "She looks from another time. Egypt perhaps. She has long black hair, a long dress. Yuki saw the wall through her."

Paula and Dee exchanged glances. "First the Café Central, now here. Coincidence? Or has whatever is in the house attached itself to us?" Dee said.

"I don't know," Paula said. She thanked the young man and he returned to his party. Yuki seemed to be calming down now. Other tourists whispered among themselves.

"Come on," Dee said. "Let's get out of here, I feel like an animal in the zoo."

That night, Paula felt rested after a long, hot bath. She climbed into bed, switched off the lamp, and closed her eyes. In the silent, dark room, she drifted into a half-awake, half-asleep state that made her limbs relax and her mind calm.

A whisper, like the gentlest of breezes, lifted tiny hairs on the back of her neck. She incorporated it into her dreamlike state. She ran through a field on a summer day, bare legs brushing against fresh, green grass. The breeze came again and she shifted position. The field vanished and she found herself in the basement.

The hieroglyphics blazed vivid scarlet. The portrait she had moved to the library was back where it had been. It didn't look right. The profile had turned to a full face. Points of light shot from the eyes like lasers. They illuminated a man. Tall, long-haired, in a black, knee-length jacket. In his hand, he held a small gold statuette representing an Egyptian god.

Set.

Paula wanted to run away, to escape this man who shouldn't be there. Couldn't be there. An impossible man with no eyes. Dead. Mummified.

Paula opened her mouth and tried to scream for help. No sound came out. The man stood still as a statue. The points of light shifted their beam away from him and onto the wall next to him. The air moved in waves. A shape began to form. Female. Long, black hair in many small braids. A deep-red silk gown. With a start, Paula recognized the woman who stood before her.

The girl in the painting. The girl with the dagger. She held it now.

She raised her arm.

"Paula! Paula! Wake up!"

Paula opened her eyes to find Dee shaking her arm.

"What? Oh my God."

"You were having a nightmare. I didn't know what else to do but wake you. You were screaming."

Paula struggled to sit up in bed, her hands shaking. "It was terrible, Dee. I was in the basement. This man... And the girl in the ceiling painting—the one I think is Arsinoe, Cleopatra's sister—she was in it, too, and I think she wanted to kill me but you woke me up. Thank God you did. It felt so *real*."

"It's all over now, so don't worry anymore about it. Do you want some tea?"

"No, I'll be fine, thanks." A sudden wave of exhaustion hit her. She yawned. "I'll go back to sleep. Hopefully with no more spooks."

Dee smiled and left her.

Despite her weariness, Paula lay awake for a long time before sleep would claim her.

The next morning, she found Dee in the library, using her laptop. She closed it and looked up as her sister came in.

"Hope you don't mind. I had to send an email to work. My boss is covering a meeting of mine in a couple of days and needed to know where some important information is stored on my computer."

"No problem. I don't have any secrets on there."

Dee sat back in her chair. "What do you fancy doing today?"

Paula looked out at the teeming rain and leaden skies. "I suggest staying under cover, so maybe a museum? The Belvedere. Feast our eyes on some great paintings and forget all this."

"Or we could just stay around here and chill out for the day. Now I'm not going back so soon, there's no major rush, and I expect you're tired after last night."

Paula shivered at the memory. "I don't want another nightmare like that in a hurry and that's for sure."

"I had one once where I was being chased by some entity I couldn't see or hear, but I knew it was there. It pursued me for miles until I reached this cliff edge. Then I had two choices, step off or turn around and face it. I felt absolutely terrified."

"What did you decide?"

"I've no idea. I woke up in a sweat, bawling my eyes out. For a few seconds, I still thought I was there."

"Why do we have them? I've never understood—"

A sudden loud crash sent Paula and Dee darting toward the kitchen.

They stopped dead at the door. "What the hell...?" Paula inched forward, stepping carefully over broken crockery and glassware. Dee followed her.

The heavy door to the basement hung drunkenly off its hinges.

Dee's voice shook. "What could have done that?"

"I have no idea."

"Paula. Stop. You're surely not going down there again."

Paula didn't reply. Some force propelled her forward. Her movements were not her own. It felt like she had invisible rope wound around her waist, tightening and squeezing the breath out of her. "For God's sake, what's happening?"

Dee's hands grabbed her from behind. "You're okay. I've got you."

The force was too strong. Dee slipped, and the two were dragged to the doorway.

Paula slammed her hands against the doorframe and pushed with every ounce of strength she could muster.

The invisible force broke its hold and the sisters staggered backward.

Paula panted, desperate to fill her lungs. "I don't know...what that was..."

"Call the agent. Tell him to get that door fixed today." Dee's eyes looked huge in her white face.

Paula called Stefan. "You need to get here right away. Something is seriously wrong. I have got broken crockery all over the floor and that basement door is not only unlocked but falling off its hinges."

The silence at the other end of the phone was deafening. Either he didn't believe her or had been shocked by what he had heard. Right now, Paula couldn't decide which.

"I'll come now."

"Fine but bring a carpenter with you. And the pest exterminator. Might as well get both jobs done now that we no longer need anyone to unlock the basement door."

Paula cut the call and her finger hovered over Phil's number. She desperately wanted to call him—needed to hear his voice—but what could he do except worry? He was so far away.

In the kitchen, she found Dee doing her best to clear up broken dishes.

"Leave that," Paula said. "Let Stefan see how bad it is."

Half an hour later, the agent arrived, with the pest exterminator.

Paula and Dee showed them into the kitchen. The exterminator let out a long whistle. Stefan looked uncomfortable. "I cannot understand how this has happened."

Paula nodded. "We can't, either. Where's the carpenter, by the way?"

"He is waiting for my call. *Gott im Himmel*." Stefan stared at the damage. Then he tentatively moved toward the shattered door. "Who could have done this?"

"That's what we would like to know," Paula said.

Stefan reached the door and peered inside. "Is there a light switch here? It is so dark."

"It doesn't work," Paula said. "You'll need a flashlight if you're going down there."

Stefan backed away into the kitchen. "No need, I think. We must call the police, unless… Have you called them already?"

"Come on, Stefan. Cut the crap. We all know this wasn't any burglary. I know perfectly well that there are things you've not told us about this house. Phone your carpenter and then I want you to tell us everything. Why is this happening? What is causing it? Everything."

Stefan shook his head. "I don't know anything. Truly. I only know the stories about this house."

"My cleaner knows stories about it. I think you know more."

Stefan made his phone call to his carpenter.

The agent and the exterminator exchanged a rapid-fire conversation. Stefan stepped aside to allow him to edge his way over to the broken door. His boots clattered on the steps leading down to the basement, fading into the distance.

"Right, tell me everything you know about this house."

Stefan looked from Paula to her sister and back again. If he hoped for sympathy from one of them, he would be sorely disappointed. He rubbed his eyes.

"This is an old house. It has seen many strange things. Dr. Quintillus—"

He didn't have chance to complete his sentence. A loud crash, a yell, the sound of heavy footsteps pounding up the steps from the basement, and the exterminator raced through the kitchen, babbling in rapid German. Stefan tried to catch him but the man shot out of the door.

"What the hell was that all about?" Paula said, her own fear reaching fever pitch while beside her, Dee blanched whiter still.

"He said there was something down there." Stefan hesitated, shaking his head. "He said it wasn't human, not an animal. I don't understand."

"That makes three of us," Paula said. "As soon as your carpenter gets here, let's get this door repaired, or replaced, and seal up that basement again. Did any of the previous tenants have these problems?"

If Stefan's eyes had grown any larger, they would have popped out of his head. "I don't know. I haven't been working for this agency for very long. Only a couple of months. I know very little about any previous tenants. All I know is that this house has a…" He struggled to find the word. "Reputation. Some say Dr. Quintillus is still here. His ghost. There is supposed to be writing on the wall of the basement. Egyptian."

"We've seen it," Paula said.

Stefan looked as if he had been shot. "You have been down there? But how is that possible? The door was locked until…" He indicated the mess.

"Not all the time," Paula said. "We found it unlocked yesterday, so we went down. Like most basements, we found it creepy, but more than that. I haven't been in any others with hieroglyphics scrawled across the wall."

Stefan's eyes grew wider. He was about to speak when they heard the scrape of a key in the kitchen door as Anna arrived. She took one look at the mess and gasped. "Whatever has happened?"

Paula told her. All the while, Anna looked hard at the estate agent.

"Have you told her? About Fräulein Zimic? About what happened to her?"

Stefan shook his head.

"Zimic? Wasn't she the one who visited Adeline Ogilvy in the care home?"

Anna nodded. "There was more to Gerda Zimic than met the eye. Her family had some criminal connections and I don't even know whether she lived here legally or not."

Stefan cleared his throat. "She bought the house from Markus von Dürnstein in 1977."

Anna nodded. "Yes, but isn't it true that the purchase wasn't in her name?"

"I don't know about that," Stefan said, and to her amazement, Paula saw his hands were trembling. He stared at the floor. Now he couldn't deny it. Stefan knew far more than he was letting on.

"If not in her name, then whose?" Paula asked.

Next to her, Dee made a tutting sound. "This gets more convoluted by the minute."

"I don't know." Stefan looked as if he would rather be anywhere than here right now.

"I think you do know," Paula said. "And I have a right to know, too."

Stefan considered this. From his expression, some battle was being conducted in his mind. He moistened his lips. "I have not seen the papers. The family has them."

"Can't you ask them? Surely they wouldn't mind their tenant knowing the name of a previous owner of this house. What harm could it do? It's not as if the owner is still alive. Didn't she die in some fire?"

Stefan looked surprised. "Who told you that?"

Paula nodded toward Anna.

"I only repeated the stories I had heard," she said.

"The story is not quite true," Stefan said, at last. "Fräulein Zimic may or may not have died in the fire. The truth that I know is that she disappeared that night and was not seen again. But her body has never been found."

"That seems to be something of a habit with people who live here."

Dee put her hand on Paula's arm. She must have sensed her sister's unease. "Look at it another way, Paula. The von Dürnsteins weren't affected. They managed to live here undisturbed for years."

Paula couldn't believe what she was hearing. Dee had been as scared as she. More so, maybe. Now she was behaving as if nothing was wrong. "Dee, they left, never to return. All because Markus von Dürnstein tampered with the building and disturbed whatever malignancy infests this place. Now, for some reason we cannot understand, this…this…thing has woken up again, and God knows what's going to happen next."

The doorbell rang and Paula jumped.

Dee made her way, with difficulty, out of the kitchen. "It'll be the carpenter. I'll let him in."

"I'll start to clear up," Anna said. "He'll need more room to work."

"Good idea," Paula said. "Thank you. Stefan, we'll go into the library and you can finish telling me what you know. Anna, tell Dee where we are."

Anna nodded, already picking up larger pieces of crockery and putting them in a heavy-duty garbage bag.

In the library, Paula faced the agent. "You may as well tell me the rest of it, because I will have my answers, even if I have to go over your head to your boss, or the family."

"Mrs. Bancroft, you put me in a very difficult position. There is confidential information. I am not permitted to tell you things the owners of this house prefer to keep to themselves."

"I am hardly going to tell the world, broadcast it on the Internet or whatever. I need to know because, for the time being at least, we have to live in this house. I need to know what I am up against."

"I can say that I do not believe you are in personal danger. You, your husband, or your sister."

"How do you know that?"

Stefan shifted from one foot to another. "Because you are not, I believe, related to Cleopatra."

Paula stared at him. "Cleopatra? You mean *the* Cleopatra?"

"Yes. Don't ask me anything more about that because I know so little."

His eyes strayed up to the painting.

Paula followed his gaze. The young woman on the bank still held her dagger. She wondered what Stefan saw.

"So, this is all to do with the infamous Dr. Quintillus," she said. "This house is infested with him."

"Yes," Stefan said, and Paula wished he hadn't sounded so definite.

She tried a different approach. "You said Fräulein Zimic didn't sign the papers purchasing this house?"

He shook his head.

"Who did?"

"I do not know the name."

"But you know something about the buyer. I can tell."

He blinked at her. "I know the buyer wasn't Austrian."

Paula now had an image of wringing out a particularly heavy, awkward blanket. "Come on, Stefan. Tell me. If the buyer wasn't Austrian, what were they?"

"British. I believe the buyer was British."

"I need a name, Stefan. I need you to get me the name and as much information as the family will let you have."

He shook his head.

"Look, if you don't give it to me, I *will* get it from somewhere. You might as well tell me. Take my word for it that I will share it only with my husband and sister, who won't tell anyone, and let's save ourselves a lot of time and effort."

A lengthy pause followed. She almost felt sorry for the man, but she couldn't back down. Not now she had come so close.

"I heard that there was something…irregular…about the purchase. About the buyer."

"Irregular? How?"

At that moment, Dee returned and slipped into the room, careful not to interrupt.

"My manager told me that, after the fire, checks were made on the identity of the buyer, and they even checked the handwriting on the signature. It matched with known signatures of that person. But it couldn't have matched."

"Why not?"

Stefan took a deep breath. "Because the person who appeared to have signed the documents had been dead for over seventy years."

Chapter 6

Hereford College, Oxford University, February 1908

The clock in the quadrangle chimed the quarter hour. Professor Andrew Charters smoothed his moustache and lit his first cigar of the day. He leaned back in comfort in his worn armchair and contemplated the flames crackling in the small fireplace. Smoke curled upward as he puffed his cigar and stretched stiff legs, feeling every one of his sixty-three years. Damn that Quintillus. He would have to demand to see him at this hour. *Demand* indeed. The man had ideas well above his dubious station. Who was he, anyway? Nobody seemed to know where he even hailed from. Hungary? The Balkans? The only Quintillus Charters could remember had been a somewhat obscure third-century Roman emperor, but he couldn't believe that this man — already ten minutes late — had been born an Italian. Emeryk. That name sounded Eastern European. The man spoke half a dozen languages, so no clue there, and as for his style of dress... Charters clicked his teeth and then wished he hadn't. The troublesome molar announced its presence again. He would have to make a trip to that sadistic dental surgeon. The thing would have to be extracted.

The door opened and the tall figure of Dr. Emeryk Quintillus strode in. Didn't the man ever knock? Charters struggled to his feet, wincing as his knees cracked. "Quintillus," he said.

Quintillus nodded to him. "Professor."

"Will you have a cigar?"

"Thank you, no. I have my own." Quintillus extracted a silver cigar case from the pocket of his deep violet coat and lit up a long, thin, black cheroot. His movements were quick, almost cat-like. It seemed to Charters he was standing one moment and a split second later had settled in an armchair opposite.

Charters took a couple of puffs of his cigar and knocked some ash off into the fire. He became aware of the archeologist's penetrating dark eyes boring into him. For once, Quintillus had removed the omnipresent stovepipe hat, and his luxuriant black hair streamed over his shoulders. His neatly trimmed beard and high cheekbones added to his exotic appearance. Charters supposed women would find him attractive. But to him, the man had an air of such menace about him as he had never previously encountered.

Charters cleared his throat. "You asked to see me?"

"I need to return to Egypt to resume my research into the missing tomb of Cleopatra." Quintillus's baritone voice held the faintest of accents.

"And when are you proposing to make this trip?"

"In the summer. June."

"Won't it be fearfully hot then?"

"The heat doesn't trouble me."

Charters looked at him. No, the heat would never dare trouble this cold man.

"And who is funding this expedition?"

"I have my own funds, and the Lorenz Museum in Berlin. I have worked with them before."

"Yes, I am aware of that. They acquired a number of artifacts that arguably should have stayed in Cairo. Your doing, I presume?"

A slow smile twitched the corners of Quintillus's mouth. "I have my methods," he said.

Charters had the sudden urge to throw the man out of his study. He seemed to contaminate it simply by being there. Nevertheless, he pressed on. "And how long do you anticipate being away?"

"Until September, maybe not quite so long. It depends on my findings."

"You have commitments here, Dr. Quintillus. I need a more precise answer."

"I am not able to give it."

"Nevertheless…"

"I am not able to give it. I shall, of course, provide regular updates on my progress."

"And where is this venture to take place?"

"Taposiris Magna, as before."

Charters exhaled loudly. "Not again. We have discussed this at great length. You're wasting your time there. If Cleopatra's tomb exists, it is almost certainly at the bottom of the Mediterranean Sea off the coast of Alexandria, along with the rest of her palace."

"That is where you are wrong, Professor. She took refuge in the great temple of Taposiris Magna and there she died, by her own hand. And there she is buried."

"So you say, but I simply cannot agree."

Quintillus spread his hands wide, palms facing upward. "Then we shall have to disagree," he said.

The silence hung like a shroud, clinging to the atmosphere, while the smoke from Charters's cigar and Quintillus's cheroot mingled and swirled together. Finally, Charters spoke.

"Why are you so convinced, despite all the evidence to the contrary?"

"I have my reasons, which I am not prepared to discuss with you at this time."

"But you still expect me to grant you the time you need for your fruitless quest?"

Charters had to stop himself from flinching at the change in Quintillus's expression. His face seemed to darken, in a way no mortal flesh should be capable of. In that moment, Charters could have believed he had the devil in him. He pushed the thought aside and waited for his adversary to respond. He didn't. The quadrangle clock chimed the half hour and still the two men stared at each other. Charters felt increasingly uncomfortable. He wanted the man out of his room. Give him what he wanted, for heaven's sake, and be done with him. At least if he went to Egypt he would no longer be Charters's responsibility. Until he returned.

"Very well, Quintillus. June to September. Final dates to be agreed."

Quintillus almost jumped to his feet. He threw his half-smoked cheroot into the fire, retrieved his incongruous hat, and nodded at Charters. "Good day, Professor."

Charters mumbled something incoherent as the door closed behind his unwanted visitor. He threw open the window, glad of the cold air that rushed in and cleansed the atmosphere. Below, he watched Quintillus stride across the lawn. A small group of students turned to watch him go by before huddling together, no doubt exchanging their opinions on the most controversial character at Oxford.

"It's not as if he has any evidence for his ridiculous claims." Charters said to his dinner companion, Professor Michael Sullivan, a fellow historian. Charters felt grateful for his company. Sanity restored. The two old friends sipped vintage port and leaned back in their chairs.

Sullivan lit a cigar. "I heard a rumor he had stolen a scroll from the archives, but I don't know how true that is."

"I wouldn't put it past him. I wouldn't put *anything* past that man."

Professor Sullivan wandered over to the fireplace and warmed his hands. At fifty-eight, he suffered from poor circulation and always had trouble keeping warm. "I don't know how he keeps his position here."

"Nobody seems to know the answer to that. It's not as if he's published many papers. Those he has aren't up to snuff. And to cap it all, the man's obsessed with Cleopatra. He barely talks of anything else."

"Have you noticed the *way* he talks about her?" Sullivan sat back down. "It's as if he knows her personally. Quite strange."

Charters shuddered. "Unhealthy. I shall be glad to see the back of him for a few months."

"Yes. I'm sure we'll all be a little easier with him out of the way for the summer. I shall look forward to it."

"Indeed."

The moon cast silvery beams across the bedroom as Charters opened his eyes. Something had woken him. A noise. He had fallen asleep reading and his book had fallen on the floor, face down, while the oil lamp still burned on his night table. He rubbed sleep-befuddled eyes and climbed out of bed. Padding over to the window, he pulled the curtain aside. The silvery glow of a full moon lit up the quadrangle; frost glittered on the grass below. Then he caught a slight movement. There, on the lawn. Someone standing, looking up, watching. That hat.

Charters dropped the curtain, stepped back, and narrowly escaped losing his footing. Why the devil would Quintillus be out there in the middle of the night, staring up at his window?

Charters shivered and retrieved his dressing gown from behind the door. He wrapped it around himself, glad of its woolen warmth. Returning to the window, he gently tweaked the curtain, hoping Quintillus wouldn't see him. But he needn't have worried. The quadrangle was empty.

"Extraordinary," he said out loud, and turned back to the room.

Behind him, Charters heard a loud hiss. He turned and saw a cobra as it reared its head. He let out a cry. The snake hissed again, its forked tongue darting in and out of its mouth. The professor dared not move. Someone must have brought it in while he slept, but who would possess such a reptile? And why target him?

Quintillus. He was vindictive enough. But Charters had given him what he asked for. Surely there could be no reason for the man to want to harm him. If he had refused, maybe, but not now.

If not Quintillus, then who? And how could he dispose of this lethal snake?

Its lithe movements gave the impression of dancing, its upper body swaying to some music only it could hear. Strangely beautiful, in a hypnotic way. If it hadn't been so deadly.

Taking care to avoid any jerky moves, Charters edged around the walls, keeping as far from the snake as possible. He reached his wardrobe and, never taking his eyes off the cobra, quietly turned the key. The door opened smoothly and the professor bent down, wishing his knees didn't creak so loudly. The snake continued its dance but returned its adversary's stare.

Charters found what he was searching for. An antique samurai sword he had picked up in Japan years earlier. His mouth dry and his heart pounding, he slid it out of its scabbard. He would only get one chance at this. If that. As a student, Charters had won fencing competitions and played for his college at Oxford, but that had been forty years ago, and he had long since hung up his mask and sheathed his rapier.

He put one tentative foot closer to the snake. The snake did not react. Maybe he could do this after all. He took another small step, and another. One more and he would be within striking distance. The cobra hissed. Sweat broke out on Charters's forehead. The palm of his right hand felt clammy against the sword hilt. He gripped it hard. Mustn't lose his nerve. He and the cobra stared at each other. Charters prayed the sword was still as sharp as he remembered. The snake must be a good ten feet long, more than half its body coiled. He would need to kill it with one fast strike or it would have him. On his travels, Charters had encountered a number of species of snake. If he was to succeed in killing this one, he needed to distract it. He untied his dressing gown and shrugged it off, moving the sword into his left hand as he did so. The snake's upper body tilted forward and Charters instinctively stepped back.

He moistened dry lips and gritted his teeth. Concentrating hard on making every move silent and nonthreatening, he slowly placed the dressing gown on the floor. The cobra followed his movements with its eyes and focused on the discarded robe.

Now. It must be now.

Using both hands, Charters raised the sword high above him and slammed it down hard on the cobra's neck as the creature struck. Its head flew to the floor, blood gushing from the wound. Charters dropped the bloody sword and sank down on the bed, panting.

It took him ten minutes before he could summon the strength to stand, find cloths to mop up the gory carpet, and an old bag to dispose of the remains.

Half an hour later, he had cleaned the room and packed up the snake, ready for disposal in the morning. Charters checked his door. Locked. He turned the key, opened the door, closed it, and locked it again. He shivered, a combination of the chill in the room and his own fears. If the door had been locked, how had Quintillus—assuming it was him—gained access?

Charters extinguished the lamp and tried, in vain, to sleep.

———

The next morning, he found Sullivan smoking his pipe in the Senior Common Room.

"Good morning, Charters. Oh, I say, your eyes are bloodshot. Have you slept at all?"

Charters shook his head and thrust the bag he was carrying at his colleague.

"What's that?"

"A cobra."

"*What?*"

Charters told him about the previous night. Sullivan listened, increasingly wide-eyed.

"And you believe Quintillus is responsible?"

"I don't see how, but I can't think of any other explanation. I saw him down in the quadrangle and then no more than a few minutes later, I was facing a cobra."

"Not even Quintillus is capable of getting through a locked door without a key."

"Do you know, Sullivan, at this moment, if you told me he could do precisely that, I would be inclined to believe you."

"Steady on, old man. Sit down. Have a brandy."

"It's far too early for brandy."

"I would make an exception this time. You've had a terrible shock. Look, sit here." He indicated a deep leather armchair. "I'll get rid of the bag for you and then we'll both have a medicinal brandy. I feel I could do with one too after what you've told me."

Too weary to protest, Charters did as his friend told him. Sullivan took the bag and undid it just enough to see the scaly, blood-soaked body. "Good God. Lucky you had that sword. If you hadn't..."

"If I hadn't, I wouldn't be here now telling you all about it. This is serious, Sullivan. An attempt has been made on my life."

"And in such a bizarre way, too."

"Really? Think about it. The cobra is indigenous to Egypt, among other places, and associated with Isis, Cleopatra's favorite goddess."

Sullivan nodded thoughtfully. "I can see your logic, but what possible reason would Quintillus have for wanting to kill you? He would gain nothing. At least you are allowing him to pursue his wild goose chase. With you gone, your successor might block him."

"True, but he would simply dispose of him too. I have long suspected Quintillus to be capable of almost anything. I sense not one ounce of humanity in the man. He knows I don't trust him and that I actively dislike him. Nor do I approve of his methods and highly questionable standards of professionalism. He may perceive me as a threat, or simply hate me enough to want to take revenge for my attempts to thwart him. Who really knows what goes on in that twisted imagination of his?"

"I still cannot fathom how he got into your room. Unless he let himself in much earlier and secreted the snake somewhere."

"That may be the case, but I'd been in my room all evening. You joined me for a glass of port after dinner and, after you left, I went directly to bed. I woke suddenly and I'm sure there had been a noise in my room."

"It couldn't have been from outside?"

Charters considered this for a moment. At the time, he hadn't been too bothered about where the noise had come from, or what it sounded like but now, reflecting back, he remembered.

"I'm almost certain someone threw gravel against my window," he said.

"Did you see them?"

"No, but I'm sure that's what woke me."

"And Quintillus was out in the quadrangle?"

"Yes."

Sullivan sighed. "I think we should see the provost. And I don't think I should dispose of the…" He shook the bag at Charters. "Evidence."

Charters slammed his fists down hard on the arms of the chair. "Good God, man, if he can try and murder me when I haven't made trouble for him, whatever do you think he'll do when he learns we were the ones to land him in Queer Street with the provost? Come to that, involving Sir Henry could put his life in danger, too, especially if it is decided that there is a case to answer and this goes to the Governing Body."

"So what do you suggest, then?"

Charters chewed his lip. "The only thing we can do is see how he reacts when he discovers his plot hasn't succeeded. I intend to go about my business as normal and say nothing of it to him or anyone else. Naturally now I shall be on my guard, and that sword won't be far from my side either. At least when I'm in my rooms."

Sullivan looked at him as if he had inexplicably grown an extra head. "And what do you propose to do with the snake?"

"Burn it."

"*Burn* it?"

"Yes. What else am I to do with it? I'm hardly going to waft it under his nose and gloat, am I? Besides, he would deny all knowledge of it."

Sullivan seemed tormented by conflicting thoughts. A frown created deep furrows on his forehead. "Very well. If that's your final word, I'll go and deal with it now before the thing starts stinking."

"Thank you, Sullivan. I appreciate your discretion."

"I can only hope you don't live to regret it."

––––––––

"Ah, Quintillus." Charters felt certain the man's eyebrows raised at the unexpected sight of him in the Senior Common Room.

"Professor," he said, returning his attention to *The Times*.

Charters lit a cigar and forced himself to sit in his usual armchair. A fire crackled in the hearth and he added an extra log. Sap sizzled and spat as the flames licked the wood.

Neither man spoke. Charters would have loved to know what thoughts ran through Quintillus's mind at that point. Presently, the man stood, folded and replaced the newspaper on a table, and left without a word.

Charters shifted in his seat. With Quintillus's departure, the atmosphere had become lighter, less dense. A sudden movement in the hearth caught his eye. An iridescent flash of metallic black and green. A beetle. Not just any beetle. Charters bent down to get a closer look at the insect, which lay motionless. Perplexed, he stood. What on earth would a scarab be doing in the Senior Common Room?

Charters glanced over to the door. Quintillus. It had to be his doing. The man was a magician, able to conjure at will. He looked down at the hearth again.

The beetle had vanished.

That night, Charters locked his door as usual and then wedged a chair under the handle. He checked his windows, ensuring they were shut tightly. Then he made a systematic check of his rooms, looking under chairs, in cupboards and under the bed. Satisfied, he made ready for bed. Lack of sleep the night before made his eyes grow heavy early. The quadrangle clock chimed ten times. Charters yawned, climbed into bed and pulled the covers over his head. Lying there in the dark, he listened. The normal peace and tranquility of Hereford College comforted him, and he soon drifted off to sleep.

He awoke in the dark, to something tickling his nose. He brushed it away without opening his eyes. It returned. Now it tried to get into his ear. He batted it away, conscious of touching something hard and shell-like. He was instantly awake and out of bed. With shaking hands, he lit his oil lamp and shone it over the sheets. The scarab darted across the mattress and out of sight.

Charters stripped the bed, but despite examining every inch, he could find no trace of the beetle. Conscious of his bare feet, he located his slippers and put his right foot in, then his left. A sharp bite sent a knife of pain tearing through his body. He tossed the slipper off and with it, the beetle. Before it could scurry away, he squashed it under his slippered right foot. Reeling with pain, he sat on the bed and lifted his foot up. His big toe had already started to swell and burn, and had turned bright red. Leaning on the furniture for support, Charters made his way to his bathroom where he ran cold water in the bath and sat on the edge, his feet immersed. The pain gradually lessened to a dull throb, but by now the toe had doubled in size. On top of the shock he had just received, a new fear asserted itself. What if that creature had given him blood poisoning?

More of Quintillus's handiwork, no doubt. Maybe he had fed the thing in under the door. Charters wrung out a facecloth, patted his feet dry and hobbled back to the bedroom. The squashed scarab still lay on the floor. Before he climbed back into bed, he stuffed some towels at the base of the door. He took a couple of aspirin and lay down, elevating his injured foot as best he could until exhaustion took over and he fell asleep.

The next morning, his toe still inflamed and throbbing, he took more aspirin and retrieved a walking stick from the wardrobe. It had come in handy when he had sprained his ankle a couple of years ago, and he once again pressed it into service.

Wearing slippers, he hobbled into the Senior Common Room to find Sullivan drinking coffee and Quintillus once again engrossed in a newspaper. At the sight of him, Sullivan set down his coffee cup. "Charters, old man, whatever's happened?"

Charters felt Quintillus's eyes burning into him. He forced his voice to remain light. "A slight accident with a beetle. I came off worst." Much as he wanted to, he avoided looking directly at Quintillus. Let the man wonder how much he had guessed.

Sullivan fussed around his friend, taking him by the arm. "Come and sit down. Tell me what you want for breakfast and I'll fetch it for you."

"Not terribly hungry this morning, old chap. Just some scrambled egg, a slice of toast, and a cup of strong coffee, please."

Quintillus stood. "You should be careful of insect bites. They can become infected."

"I don't remember mentioning I had been bitten. Merely that I had had an accident with one."

Quintillus didn't even blink. "I assumed from the way you were walking. My advice holds true. Be very careful. The consequences can be fatal."

He left.

Sullivan placed Charters' breakfast in front of him. "What do you suppose that's all about?"

"A warning. Clear as a bell. I have just been warned not to meddle with him or suffer the consequences."

"That's hardly a warning. That's a threat. We have to see the provost now. He can't get away with it."

"No, Sullivan."

His friend flinched at the vehemence punctuating his words.

"Oh, Sullivan, I do apologize. That was unforgiveable of me. Especially after your kindness, but I must insist. No good will come of reporting this. The man is sly, manipulative, and highly intelligent. Whatever you do to him, you receive back threefold—at least. Best leave well alone. I have a feeling if we do so, he'll think he's made his point and move on."

Sullivan poured himself more coffee.

"For your sake, I hope you're right."

Over the next week, Charters's toe gradually returned to its normal size and color. It stopped throbbing and he could consign the walking stick to the back of the wardrobe.

Nothing more happened, and even Sullivan began to acknowledge that Charters had probably been right. February became March, and with it came the end of term. The students left the college for their Easter vacation and Charters settled down to his comfortable non-term routine of research and working on his latest paper on Babylonian culture.

Sullivan had left for a couple of weeks at his home in the Cotswolds and, not having a great deal in common with his fellow academics who chose to remain at Hereford, Charters spent most of his time alone, in his room or in the library. Only at mealtimes did he join the others when, three times a day, he would encounter Quintillus. He too had little to say. One such lunchtime, Charters was a few minutes late in arriving. Quintillus had eaten and left shortly after. A science professor—Longworth—tapped him on the shoulder as he ate his cottage pie. "May I join you, Charters?"

"By all means." He indicated a chair and the elderly professor sat, with some difficulty.

"That chap—Quintillus—one of yours, I believe."

"Yes."

"What do you know about him?"

"Not a great deal, to be honest. I know he holds a clutch of degrees from various European universities and his research area is ancient Egypt, more particularly Cleopatra's Egypt. Why do you ask?"

The professor moved closer and spoke in a hushed voice. "The damnedest thing. The chap has rooms adjoining mine and I often hear him. Chanting. Can't understand a word he says but it's definitely chanting. Not only that, there are these queer smells. Lilies sometimes, and that's not too bad, but other times, to put no finer point on it, there are occasions where I would swear he had a corpse in there, however ridiculous that may sound."

"No, Professor, I'm afraid it doesn't sound ridiculous at all. Not to me."

"I don't want to be the harbinger of doom, old man, but I think you've got a problem with that one. How long has he been here?"

"Three years. Three *long* years. I wasn't aware he had taken rooms. I thought he lived in lodgings somewhere in town. Although, if I'm being honest, I don't think I ever gave his abode much thought."

"He only moved next door at the beginning of term. Since then, I've been plagued by all sorts of annoying events. The chanting and the smells I mentioned. Then one day, half a dozen beetles suddenly appeared in my hearth. Goodness alone knows how they got in. Looked foreign, too. I reported the infestation but blow me if they hadn't all disappeared when the chap turned up to fumigate. Of course, I probably shouldn't blame him for that. I mean, how could he cause a plague of beetles?" Longworth threw back his snowy head and guffawed. He stopped short. Charters knew it was because of the expression on his face.

"You do think he's responsible, don't you?"

"I believe he is very dangerous when crossed. I don't know how or why, and I have no real evidence to go on, but I believe he is determined to do me harm. A cobra appeared in my room and a beetle bit me rather badly. In both cases, I was able to dispose of the creature concerned, but you tell me what a cobra is doing here, in the residences of Oxford University?"

"My dear man, you must report your fears to the provost. At once."

"If I believed it would do any good, I would. As things stand, it could only serve to make things worse for me, and possibly others. He is off on a dig in Egypt in June. At least that gives me the summer to decide what to do about him."

Longworth shifted uncomfortably. He smoothed his moustache. "All I can do is wish you well, and keep you informed of any other strange activities."

"Thank you, I would appreciate that."

"Don't mention it. Take care of yourself, old man."

"Good gracious, Lizzie. I didn't expect to see you here." Charters stepped back to allow his niece to enter his study.

The slim girl with shining hazel eyes almost skipped in. Her attractive face was further enhanced by the broad smile that gave the impression she hadn't a care in the world.

Charters indicated a chair by the fire and she arranged herself on it.

"To what do I owe this pleasure, my dear?"

"Didn't Papa tell you? I'm studying ancient history here—at Lady Rhona Ray College."

Charters searched his memory. "No, I don't believe he did. I'm sure I would have remembered. But surely you haven't just arrived? It's the end of Hilary."

"Oh no, I started at Michaelmas, but I've been so busy with lectures and studies. And, all right, I confess, there have been some social events, too. I did pop over a couple of times, but I never caught you in. I suppose I should have left a note, but it didn't occur to me. Sorry, Uncle."

She smiled her brilliant smile and won Charters over. She'd always had the power to do that, ever since she'd been a tiny baby, all pink and giggling. His only niece and goddaughter. Why on earth hadn't Ernest told him? Of course, his brother was a noted eccentric. He frequently went out of his house in all weathers without a hat or coat, and now Charters came to think of it, he couldn't actually remember when the two had last exchanged correspondence, let alone talked to each other. He made a mental note to rectify that. It wasn't as if there had been any bad blood between them.

"How is your father?" he asked.

Lizzie rolled her eyes. "Oh, just as vague as ever. Always writing down mathematical equations. Something to do with pi, I think. He's trying to solve it, or prove it, or whatever they call it. All I know is there are papers all over the house awash with the most fearfully long rows of numbers. It's pretty much all he talks about."

"And your mother?" An image of a pretty woman with brown hair, not unlike Lizzie, sprang into his mind—the only thing he and his brother had ever really disagreed on and fallen out over. Charters saw her first, but his brother won the prize. Even now, twenty-five—no thirty—years on, he still felt a pang of regret for what might have been. Since then no other woman had even come close to the standard set by the enigmatic Flora Harmsworth.

The smile had left Lizzie's face. "She doesn't approve."

"Of what?"

"Me coming here. To Oxford. To study. She thinks it is quite unladylike and that I should be staying at home, going to parties and surrounding myself with eligible young men. I'm afraid we had words about it and we're not getting along very well. When I do go home, which isn't often, I try and steer clear of her as much as possible. Mealtimes are a bit of a strain. She and I are polite in a forced kind of way and Papa hasn't got a clue what's going on, so he sits there staring at his soup."

"Good gracious, what a picture you paint."

Back came the smile. "It'll sort itself out with time. I think she's finally beginning to understand that I won't change my mind. I am determined to complete my studies, even if—being a woman—I'm not allowed to graduate. Anyway, I've come to talk to you about something else. Do you know Dr. Emeryk Quintillus?"

From her reaction, Charters guessed his face must have shown the sudden wave of dread that passed through him.

"Why do you want to know?"

"I have attended some of his lectures. He's fascinating."

"Keep away from him."

"What? Why?"

"He's a very dangerous man. Probably the most dangerous I have ever had the misfortune to meet."

"Are we talking about the same man? Tall. Very long, dark hair. Often wears a stovepipe hat?"

"There could only be one Emeryk Quintillus. Lizzie, please, for your own sake, stop attending his lectures."

Lizzie's mouth set in a firm line, exactly as her mother's used to do. "I'm sorry, Uncle, but Dr. Quintillus's lectures are by far the most interesting. I'm learning so much from him."

"There are other equally learned academics. You're welcome to attend my lectures if you wish."

"Thank you, Uncle, but I would hate any of the other students to think I was receiving preferential treatment."

"Not at all, Lizzie. I would make the same offer to any of your new friends. Promise me you'll stay away from that man. No good will come of it."

Lizzie hesitated for one moment, then her jaw set. In one swift movement, she leaped to her feet. "Uncle, I don't wish to defy you, or for us to fall out about this, but I'm afraid I cannot do as you ask. I shall continue to attend Dr. Quintillus's lectures, which I find enjoyable and informative and—"

"Good God, girl! You're attracted to the man!

Her deepening blush confirmed his worst fears.

"And what of it? He's highly educated, extremely well read, and has firsthand experience of archeological digs in Egypt—"

"Apart from everything I've already said about the man, he's old enough to be your father. Maybe even your grandfather."

Lizzie's incredulous stare was followed by a hoot of laughter. "Grandfather? Brother, maybe."

"My dear child—"

"I am *not* a child. And now you're beginning to sound like my mother."

"My dear…Lizzie, I have no idea exactly how old Quintillus is, but I do know he has been supplying artifacts to a museum in Berlin since the 1870s. So, unless he started doing so in his teens, he must be at least sixty, and I don't need to be the mathematician your father is to work out that he could easily be old enough to be your grandfather. You're twenty years old. What are you thinking of?"

Lizzie blinked a few times. His revelation seemed to have caught her off guard. She recovered herself. "Nevertheless, I shall not stop attending his lectures. I am learning more from him than anyone else. It's not as if I'm doing anything immoral."

She meant it. She started making for the door. Charters made one last desperate plea. "Lizzie, I must tell you that I have every reason to conclude that Quintillus means me harm."

"You'll stop at nothing, will you?"

"He knows I don't trust him and could be obstructive to whatever nefarious plans he might have. He would prefer me out of the way."

"Oh, now I've heard everything." She put her slim, gloved hand on the doorknob. "Good-bye, Uncle. I won't trouble you again while I'm here."

"No, Lizzie, don't leave like this…"

But she already had.

Chapter 7

Lizzie Charters strode purposefully across the quadrangle, ignoring the tears that threatened to spill over onto her cheeks. How could Uncle Andrew say such things? The man he was raging about certainly wasn't the Dr. Quintillus she knew. She glanced at her fob watch. Ten minutes before two. She had arranged to meet with Dr. Quintillus at two thirty in the library at Hereford College. He had said he had a matter of importance to discuss with her.

Lizzie quickened her step. She had plenty of time but she wanted to arrive early, tidy herself up, and make sure her hair hadn't escaped from its hastily arranged bun.

She entered the library at ten past two. Looking around its vast emptiness, she was glad there was no one else around. She would have the doctor all to herself. A delicious thrill shot up her body and lodged in her throat. Sixty years old indeed! She doubted he could be more than forty. Anyway, they had a purely professional relationship. She dreamed of more, but the chance to work with such a great man was enough. At least for now. She smiled to herself and sat at a large table.

At precisely two thirty, the door opened and the tall man strode in. He removed his hat and sat opposite her. She had to avert her gaze from him momentarily. Those dark eyes of his burned into her, almost as if they could read her mind. Dr. Quintillus rarely smiled, which added another ingredient to his mystique, along with the hypnotic quality of his voice. She could happily float away on it, lulled into a peaceful, caressing slumber. He spoke now, and she had to concentrate hard to hear his words. Not that he spoke indistinctly. It was… Her uncle was right. She had grown more than a little attracted to this charismatic and unusual man.

"Thank you for coming here this afternoon, Miss Charters. I trust you are well?"

He's just asked me a question. Lizzie's cheeks burned. "I am very well, thank you, sir. And you?"

He nodded and spread his hands on the table. Lizzie noted the long, slender fingers. The hands of an artist or a musician, rather than someone who dug in the sands of Egypt.

"I have a proposition for you. I wish to carry out an experiment. A truly important experiment of great historical significance. To do this I need an assistant. Will you be my assistant, Miss Charters?"

If he had asked her to marry him, she couldn't have been more taken aback. Unable to trust herself to speak, she nodded.

"Good. I am to travel to Egypt in June. To a site near Alexandria. I believe that once I am there, I will make a discovery of such significance, it would astound the academic world. If they should ever find out about it." He leaned forward. "Miss Charters, I do not intend that anyone should know about it. Apart from myself and a select few of my choosing. Will you be one of those?"

Again she nodded, her cheeks burning ever stronger.

Quintillus leaned back. "Excellent. You will need to equip yourself for the desert, where it is burning hot at the height of the day and freezing cold at night. When you are not on the site, accommodation will be in a hotel of quality in Alexandria, where you will enjoy excellent food and wine. The camp is much more basic, so I would suggest you think carefully about the clothes you take with you."

Lizzie regained her voice. "This dig. Is it at Taposiris Magna?" Dr. Quintillus had told them of the great, ruined temple a few weeks earlier.

"It is."

"And this discovery… Is it connected to Cleopatra?"

"You are very bright, Miss Charters. And correct. Now that you have guessed, I must ask you to swear you will not divulge this information to anyone. Certain academic staff at this university are aware of my theories and dismiss them. I believe your uncle is one of the skeptics."

Lizzie flushed. She hoped he didn't ask her about her contact with the professor. She said nothing. Quintillus's eyes searched hers. Whether they found what they were looking for or not, she couldn't tell. He moved on.

"We will be away from the university for most of the summer. It should prove to be an exciting experience for you."

"Yes indeed, Dr. Quintillus. I am most grateful for this opportunity."

"I have been impressed by your quick brain and ability to absorb facts with speed and accuracy. You also have an intuitive quality about you which could prove most helpful to me."

"Thank you."

"Your admiration for Gertrude Bell's work in Arabia shows character."

"She's a great pioneer for aspiring female archeologists like me to follow."

"Indeed." Dr. Quintillus rose from the table. "And now, Miss Charters, I must go. Have a pleasant afternoon."

He picked up his hat, replaced it on his head, and left her alone, her heart pounding. Only after he'd gone did the realization of what she had agreed to do dawn on her. Not only had she ignored her uncle's warnings, she had said she would go to Egypt for three months, alone with a man she hardly knew.

Lizzie sat for a few minutes, taking in what had just happened. Something gleamed metallically on the floor right where the doctor had been sitting. She stood, went around to the other side of the table and bent down.

A large beetle lay motionless on the floor—its carapace black with a brilliant green iridescence. As she watched, mesmerized, it gradually disintegrated until nothing but a small pile of gray ash remained.

A sigh wafted the tiny hairs on the back of her neck, and out of the corner of her eye she would swear she saw a movement. Like a cat leaping. She walked up and down the rows of bookcases, the only sound coming from her boots as they tapped along the wooden floor. There was no cat. She must have imagined it.

But she wasn't imagining the discarded cat's whisker on the table.

Chapter 8

Lizzie struggled with the lock on her trunk. With one final push, the key turned stiffly and snapped into place.

"You're all packed then?" Her roommate, a no-nonsense young woman called Marcia Goodman-Stowe, lit a cigarette as Lizzie arranged her hat, which she then skewered with a lethal-looking hatpin.

Seeing her reflection in the wall mirror, Lizzie nodded. "Look, I know you don't approve, Marcia. Neither does my mother or my uncle, but this is an opportunity of a lifetime. How many other people get a chance to work with an eminent archeologist on what could prove to be the find of the century?"

"That you're not allowed to talk about. Don't you think that's a little strange, even for Dr. Quintillus?"

"He has his reasons. He doesn't want the publicity. As soon as the newspapers get wind of an exciting find, they're all over the dig. It's happened before. It could jeopardize everything."

"Who's financing it? The university?"

"Dr. Quintillus has independent means."

"He's financing it all himself, then?" Marcia whistled through her teeth.

"I believe the Lorenz Museum in Berlin is providing some funds, and he has his own wealth."

"Inherited?"

"I really don't know, Marcia. It's none of my business." Lizzie's anger rose. The more Marcia, her mother and her uncle tried to dissuade her, the more determined she had become to see this through. She wished they would all accept her decision and let her enjoy the moment.

Marcia stubbed out her cigarette and put her hand on Lizzie's arm. "Don't be defensive, Lizzie. If it was anyone other than Quintillus I wouldn't be so apprehensive." She let her hand drop away. "But then, anyone other than Quintillus probably wouldn't have made such an outrageous suggestion."

Lizzie balled her fist in exasperation. "For heaven's sake! Anyone would think we were running away to have an illicit affair."

Marcia looked at her steadily. "Aren't you?"

"How could you even think that?"

"Because over these past months, I've come to know you rather well. I've seen the way your eyes shine whenever you talk about him. And you talk about him a lot."

"All right, he's an attractive, enigmatic man, I'll admit that, but he is first and foremost an archeologist, and I have deep respect for that. I am going along as his assistant. Nothing more or less than that."

"Let's hope he thinks the same way."

"I'm quite certain he does. He has never made one improper suggestion to me."

"Hmm." Marcia looked unconvinced. "You're aware of his obsession with Cleopatra?"

"Yes."

"Just be careful, that's all. There's something odd about that man. Much as I enjoy his lectures, I always feel he's somewhere else. Not in the room with us."

Lizzie laughed. "That's crazy. Of course he's in the room with us."

"I've been talking to a few of the others and they agree with me. He makes us feel uncomfortable. It seems he makes all of us feel that way except you. I find myself wondering why."

"Maybe because I'm not prone to flights of fancy as much as you are. Mass hysteria, that's all it is."

"I hope you're right, Lizzie. I truly do. Three months in the desert with that man is not an experience I would be looking forward to, whatever the prize at the end."

The mantelpiece clock chimed the hour. "Gracious, I'd better get going." Lizzie planted a peck on Marcia's cheek, picked up her overnight case, and opened the door. "They'll come for the trunk within the hour. I'll send you a postcard from Egypt."

"Just be careful, Lizzie," Marcia said to the closing door.

———

Dr. Quintillus helped Lizzie into the carriage and the driver urged the horse forward. Excitement bubbled up inside her as they set off. This promised to be the adventure of a lifetime, and she couldn't wait to get started. Opposite her, the doctor read a slim volume. She couldn't see the title.

The carriage slowed as they approached the rail station to catch the Southampton train. The sea journey to Alexandria would take two weeks. Two weeks in the company of Dr. Quintillus. Whatever she might have said to the others, the prospect of being alone with the man she admired above all others sent a delicious tingle of pleasure up Lizzie's spine.

They spoke little beyond exchanging pleasantries on the train journey to Southampton. Dr. Quintillus read most of the time, while Lizzie preferred to study the view from the window as they passed through sunny green countryside and stopped at places such as Reading and Winchester. They arrived at the busy port and alighted in bright sunshine, a gentle breeze alleviating what could have been a blazing hot day.

Once boarded on the ship that would take them to their destination, Lizzie and Quintillus made their way to their cabins. They weren't adjoining, but at least they were on the same deck.

"Join me for dinner, Miss Charters. I believe we dine at seven."

"Thank you, Dr. Quintillus. Is it formal?"

"I believe so."

In her cabin, Lizzie tossed her case on the bed. The heat made her feel uncomfortably damp, so she opened the porthole and leaned out, trying to catch any breath of air that wafted her way. A knock sounded at her door.

"Your trunk, Miss." The cabin boy had to be younger than she was. Certainly shorter. She thanked him, gave him a small tip and then began the business of unpacking.

She checked her watch. Four thirty. Time for a much-needed bath and a rest before dinner.

At two minutes before seven, a soft knock on her door announced Quintillus's arrival. He had dressed elegantly in formal evening attire, his long hair neatly combed. A ghost of a smile flicked the corners of his lips, and Lizzie felt he had just showered her with compliments. She knew she looked her best. The lilac cotton-voile dress, trimmed with lace at the neck and short, puffed sleeves, showed off her slender arms and hands. She had piled up her hair and it gleamed in the evening sunlight. Little diamond earrings twinkled in her ears.

She walked with Dr. Quintillus, proud to be at his side. They dined on vichyssoise and roast sirloin of beef, followed by cranberry tart. The doctor ordered a bottle of Chablis, and the waiter kept their glasses topped up so that, by the end of the meal, Lizzie felt quite lightheaded.

Dr. Quintillus placed his napkin on the table. "When we arrive in Alexandria, the hotel is near the harbor. I trust it will be satisfactory for you. I have stayed there on previous occasions and been comfortable."

His eyes lingered a little longer than necessary. Lizzie wondered if the wine had affected him, too, but he gave no other sign of it.

"For now though, I shall turn in early this evening. I have work to do in my cabin." He stood and inclined his head a little before leaving her alone.

Lizzie drained her glass before she, too, retired to her cabin. The wine, which had initially stimulated her, now made her sleepy. She bowed to the inevitable, undressed, put on an ankle-length white cotton nightdress, and pulled her sheets back.

The bed welcomed her and she fell asleep within minutes, only to awaken some hours later, before dawn. The ship sailed smoothly on, only a faint sound of the ocean splashing the sides filtered in through the open porthole.

Lizzie heard a slight noise, opened her eyes, and froze. Over by the door, a faint greenish glow pulsed and grew stronger. Lizzie hardly dared breathe. Within the glow, a smoky, indistinct image writhed and twisted. The glow moved, slowly. Came closer to her. Lizzie shrank back in her bed, curled into a fetal position, and prayed. *Make it go away. Please make it go away.*

The glow inched forward. No more than six feet away.

Lizzie closed her eyes, every muscle trembling, every nerve twitching.

Whispers. Must be coming from the glow. They spoke in ancient tongues. Not Latin. Much older. Lizzie couldn't tell what they were saying, but it didn't matter.

Make them go away.

She gritted her teeth.

The voices stopped.

Nothing happened.

She stayed still as seconds ticked by.

Still nothing.

Lizzie opened her eyes. The glow had gone.

The next morning, it seemed like a bad dream. Should she share it with the doctor? No, better not to. Of what possible interest were her nightmares to him?

Directly after breakfast, he again made his excuses and left her alone. This settled into a pattern for the rest of the voyage. They met for meals and nothing else. The rest of the time, she generally remained on deck, in the shade, reading, while he worked in his cabin.

Squalls in the Bay of Biscay emptied the dining room and sent passengers racing for their cabins or the rails. Lizzie thanked providence for giving her a strong constitution as she steadied herself amidships, but Dr. Quintillus barely seemed to notice the weather.

"May I ask what you're working on, Doctor?" she asked at dinner one evening.

He finished chewing his salmon before replying. "Preparation for the dig."

"Is there anything I can do to assist?"

"No. Take the opportunity to enjoy the sea air and relax while you can. All too soon you will wish you were back here. You will find the desert heat relentless."

"I'm sure the excitement of it all will outweigh any discomfort I may feel."

Dr. Quintillus nodded.

———

Their arrival in Alexandria brought hordes of Egypt's poor swarming around them. Members of the ship's company ordered them away while porters and stewards battled with trunks and a seething mass of passengers. For a few minutes, Lizzie wondered how they would ever sort out their luggage and get away from the insistent pushing and cries of *"Baksheesh! Baksheesh!"*

One small child of indeterminate sex tugged hard on Lizzie's purse. She wrenched it back. The child scowled at her and thrust a small, filthy hand in her face. *"Baksheesh!"*

Quintillus appeared at her side and, to Lizzie's astonishment, clouted the child across the head. The boy took one look at the eccentrically dressed man and a look of terror flashed across his dirty face. He sped off, disappearing into the crowds.

"Come with me," Quintillus said. Lizzie followed, speechless.

At the sight of the tall man in the stovepipe hat, the horde seemed to melt away to let them pass. In no time at all, they were in a horse-drawn carriage on their way to the hotel.

Lizzie's first sight of the majestic Hotel Regal Imperial took her breath away.

Built in the Gothic revival style, its majestic architecture dominated its surroundings as it towered up into the clear blue sky.

Immediately when their carriage stopped, uniformed staff appeared to help them out, take their luggage, and check them in. Lizzie's shoes sank into the luxurious rugs of the lobby. She longed to release her aching feet from their constraining leather and allow her cramped toes to be kissed by the exquisitely soft pile.

This time their rooms were next to each other, albeit without a connecting door.

Lizzie unpacked her trunk, which had miraculously arrived before her. The large, polished, dark wood wardrobe slid silently open as soon as she turned the key. Lizzie quickly took out the clothes she would not need in the desert. After all, they would hardly be dining in style there. Out came her evening gowns and cotton day dresses. Dr. Quintillus had reserved their rooms in the hotel for the duration of their stay in Egypt. Much as she longed to be in the thick of it, Lizzie was under no illusions; conditions onsite would be primitive at best. It would be comforting to know that a welcoming bed and relaxing bath awaited her back here.

She smoothed out the creases on each of her dresses and hung them carefully on their hangers, until all that was left were the much more serviceable, practical clothes she would need in the days and weeks she was on the dig.

She opened the French windows, and the aroma of the sea drifted in. A gentle breeze soothed her, and the waters of the blue Mediterranean twinkled in the bright sunshine.

That night, she lay with her windows open. Tomorrow, she would go to Taposiris Magna for the first time. The excitement had become almost too much to bear.

Lizzie closed her eyes and turned on her side. The cool breeze wafted the drapes and brought the faint strains of someone chanting. A scent of lilies seeped in. In Lizzie's pre-sleep state of semiconsciousness, a shadow crossed her mind and brought her awake, just as it descended on her.

Her eyes opened to a cloak of darkness scented with lilies and an unpleasant trace of something long dead. It held her fast in an invisible grip. She struggled to free herself and couldn't. Whatever held her down exerted a powerful force. She tossed from side to side, calling for help. Dr. Quintillus must come. Surely he could hear her.

The whispers. As on the ship. A woman's raucous laugh. Lizzie strained and pushed. She kicked out.

The cloak lifted. A nightmare. It must have been, but…

A man stood in her room, silhouetted against the window.

Lizzie screamed.

"Miss Charters."

"Dr. Quintillus? But how did you get in here?"

"I heard you crying out and crossed from my balcony to yours. What has caused you such distress?"

"I…" How could she tell him she had experienced another nightmare? One that seemed so real…

"I am so sorry to have disturbed you," she said, pulling the sheet up to her chin.

"Not at all. I have been working on last-minute preparations for tomorrow, but they are finished now. Are you quite recovered?"

"Yes, I'm fine. Thank you so much for coming to my assistance."

Dr. Quintillus inclined his head and unlocked the door. "You should lock this as soon as I have gone, Miss Charters. You don't want any other visitors tonight."

"No indeed, Doctor." Lizzie waited until he had shut the door, then lit a candle by her bed, padded over, and turned the key.

These bad dreams seemed so real. She had never previously been one for poor or troubled sleep. Maybe it was all the excitement. She climbed back into bed and watched in disbelief as a single white feather floated down from the ceiling. It landed gracefully on her bed. She retrieved it and examined it in the candlelight. Quite a large feather. It must have come from a sizable bird. She put it on her bedside table and covered it with her book. Tomorrow she would ask Dr. Quintillus about it. She blew out her candle and fell into a deep, untroubled sleep.

She forgot about the feather until she was ready to go down for breakfast, but however hard she searched the table and then the room, she could find no trace of it. Somehow it had vanished from beneath her book. Supposing it hadn't, though? Supposing she had dreamt that as well?

Lizzie shook her head and opened her door.

Chapter 9

Lizzie shaded her eyes, grateful for the broad-brimmed hat and scarf that kept the blazing sun off her head. She had dressed in an outfit she felt sure her heroine, Gertrude Bell, would have approved of—indeed, she had pioneered the style. A long, light-brown wraparound covered a matching divided skirt. When mounted on horseback, she would be able to sit astride in the masculine style rather than the more traditional feminine sidesaddle. The whole ensemble felt much more practical and comfortable. So what if she attracted disapproval? There probably wouldn't be any other women on the dig anyway. In any case, when she walked, the wraparound concealed the divided skirt.

She had selected a cream-colored cotton shirt, wide-brimmed straw hat and, to cover her neck and shoulders, she secured a kaffiyeh—the traditional Arab scarf. It would protect her from the relentless rays of the sun, which, she knew from her research, could easily penetrate a cotton shirt. On her feet, she wore good-quality soft leather boots, both for comfort and protection.

For the cold evenings, she had packed a fur coat and some warm sweaters. She would sleep in a muslin sleeping bag, which would also protect her from sand flies and other biting insects.

A less-than-comfortable carriage ride took them the thirty miles from Alexandria to Taposiris Magna, arriving in late afternoon.

Lizzie stepped down from the carriage and took in the towering, ruined stone pylons and the sheer scale of the temple. "It's magnificent," she said.

"Indeed," Dr. Quintillus replied.

All around them, Egyptian laborers dressed in an array of colorful gallabiyahs, chipped, dug, and scraped the rocky ground as they sang. In the distance, a rotund man wearing a pith helmet and dressed appropriately for the conditions scurried toward them. He flapped a large white handkerchief.

He reached them, panting hard. "Herr Doktor," he managed.

"Miss Charters, this is my assistant from the Lorenz Museum—Max Dressler."

Lizzie held out her hand, grateful for the glove that separated the man's sweaty palm from hers.

The man acknowledged her. "Fräulein. Herr Doktor, I believe we are getting close. One of the men found this an hour ago."

He reached in his pocket and held out a small gold amulet featuring a winged scarab. Dr. Quintillus handed it to Lizzie. "Your first fresh find, Miss Charters."

Lizzie took the precious artifact in her right hand and gently turned it over. Hieroglyphics adorned the reverse. "I can't read these, I'm afraid. But this is so beautiful." Reluctantly, she handed it back to the doctor. He examined the inscription.

"This is Cleopatra's cartouche. Where did you find it?"

"I will take you there. Come. Please." Dressler urged them to follow as he scuttled away.

A greater concentration of laborers was hard at work in this section of the temple. They had dug down and uncovered what looked suspiciously like a step.

Dr. Quintillus bent and stroked the stone. Lizzie watched, fascinated, as a change came over his face. His eyes took on a brilliance that eclipsed their normal darkness, while he continued to stroke the stone as if it were a precious cat.

He turned to Lizzie. "Can you feel her presence?"

"I'm sorry. I..." Lizzie didn't know what to say next. The doctor seemed in some sort of trance.

He stood and brushed sand off his trousers. Lizzie marveled at how he didn't appear to feel the heat. He still wore a long black jacket and his familiar stovepipe hat as he had done at Oxford. Dr. Quintillus took out his cigar case and removed a cheroot.

"A few more weeks and we shall succeed. I know it. Her presence is all around us in this place. Your uncle will have to eat his words, Miss Charters."

Lizzie nodded. Maybe then Uncle Andrew would realize how wrong he had been about Dr. Quintillus.

But the doctor didn't intend anyone to know about his find, so how would that happen?

Lizzie pushed the thoughts to the back of her mind.

"Carry on with the work, Dressler. I want armed guards placed all around the temple. If anyone trespasses, order them to shoot to kill, do you understand? Nothing can get in the way of our work."

"Yes, Herr Doktor."

That brought Lizzie up sharp. Shoot to kill? And by his tone, he meant it. She brushed aside a cold wave of fear that threatened to spoil her otherwise perfect day.

"Come with me, Miss Charters," the doctor said. "I want to show you some of the earlier finds."

He led her to a tent a few yards away. Two Egyptians held rifles, barring the way. As soon as Lizzie and Dr. Quintillus reached the tent, they stepped aside to let them through.

"I pay them well," the doctor said to Lizzie. "The finds are safer here than in a bank vault in Cairo."

Seeing their size and the expressions on the faces of the guards, Lizzie didn't doubt it for a second.

Dr. Quintillus unlocked a trunk secured with two enormous padlocks. He lifted the lid and Lizzie stared down at alabaster statuettes, representations of Isis, Sekhmet—the warlike goddess with the head of a lioness—and the jackal-headed god, Anubis. Lizzie reached in and picked up a perfect amulet with a representation of Isis in its center.

"Beautiful, isn't it?" he said.

"Incredible. All of this has been found here?"

"Yes. There is much more we haven't found yet, but now, in days or weeks, we will discover what man has sought for centuries. The tomb of Queen Cleopatra."

Lizzie's mouth went dry. She had wondered, certainly, given his obsession with the long-dead queen, but this would be the epitome for any archeologist—to find the most sought-after tomb in the world—and he wanted to keep it quiet?

"Dr. Quintillus, are you sure? Could she really be here?"

"It is the only place that makes sense. I know practically every other historian and archeologist believes she lies at the bottom of the sea, but I have long believed that when it became impossible for her to stay in Alexandria, she fled for the sanctuary of this great temple. When I discovered the scroll, I had my proof. The author wrote it shortly after her death, and his directions placed her here."

"So, Mark Antony will also be buried here."

Quintillus's expression changed. His eyes grew darker. "He may be." The words were clipped and curt. If they had been discussing a live woman, Lizzie would have suspected jealousy, but surely he couldn't be envious of a lover who had been dead for two thousand years. Especially when the object of his affections was a mummified corpse. Lizzie shuddered and hoped Dr. Quintillus didn't notice.

He shut the trunk with a loud slam and locked it, replacing the keys in his waistcoat pocket. Then, without a word, he marched out of the tent, leaving Lizzie trailing behind.

"Dressler."

His assistant stepped forward, sweating even more profusely as the sun blazed down.

"Yes, Herr Doktor?"

"I want you to ensure no one leaves this site, and I mean no one. You included. Only Miss Charters and I will be permitted to come and go. Do you understand?"

"Yes, Herr Doktor. It shall be so."

"Supplies will be delivered daily and you are to take personal charge of them. Anyone caught trying to leave will be shot. Understood?"

Again the flash of fear at hearing the doctor give that order. But again, Lizzie dismissed it. Dr. Quintillus was preserving irreplaceable artifacts. Being on the verge of making possibly the greatest discovery in centuries, he *had* to protect the site's integrity at all costs.

Dressler nodded nervously. A nerve twitched at the corner of his left eye, and Lizzie felt almost sorry for him.

"Come, Miss Charters," the doctor said. "I will show you your tent and you can unpack. Then we can discuss my plans."

Her trunk had already been placed in her tent by the man who would attend to her needs while she was in camp. He told her his name was Abbas and showed her an adjoining tent where she would bathe. A canvas bath stood ready for her use, and a pile of fluffy white towels lay on a folding table nearby. In her sleeping tent, a camp bed had been made up with blankets to keep out the night chill. A small desk and folding chair, an occasional table, and a mirror attached somewhat haphazardly to the tent wall formed the remaining furniture, along with a rail for her to hang her clothes. Inside the tent, the atmosphere nearly stifled her.

The tall Egyptian sensed her discomfort. He spoke in perfect English. "It will be more pleasant when the sun goes down. Then you will be glad of the blankets."

He offered her peppermint tea, for which she had acquired a taste. She thanked him and unpacked the remainder of her clothes.

A few minutes later, she joined Dr. Quintillus in his tent. He had tied the flaps open, and a slight breeze dried the sweat that had formed droplets on her brow. She sat on the only other chair and sipped her tea.

The doctor continued writing penciled notes in a small black notebook he always carried. While he wrote, Lizzie reflected in more detail on the incident earlier with Dressler. She had never thought Quintillus capable of murder. In fact, she had never given such a matter any thought at all. But twice today he had instructed a member of his team to shoot anyone transgressing his rules. He seemed to have no difficulty in delivering such an order, either. Despite her earlier conviction that he was only taking all necessary precautions to protect the site, a chill passed through her body.

Dr. Quintillus attached his pencil to the notebook and slid the slim volume into his inside pocket. He took a sip of tea. "You remember I spoke to you of an experiment I wished you to participate in?"

Lizzie nodded.

"It is time to begin that experiment. There is much preparation to do before we can fully execute it. Are you ready to commence?"

"What do you wish me to do?"

"You? Nothing for now. Your task will come later. First, I must prepare the way for you."

"The way?"

"Yes. You will see."

That look in his eyes. Always his eyes. They attracted her, but at that moment, they terrified her.

"Dr. Quintillus, what is this experiment?"

"The time for questions will come later. Much later. If at all. When the time comes, you will find you have all the answers you need. Until then, you must trust me." Unexpectedly, he leaned forward and took her wrist. His skin felt warm and dry. He stroked the back of her hand and her fears melted away. The now-familiar longing for more intimate physical contact with him flooded her, and she wondered if he could sense that. But he said nothing, patted her hand, and leaned back.

Lizzie moistened her dry lips.

"Now, Miss Charters, I suggest you return to your tent and rest before dinner. The heat is tiring and can consume all your energy."

"Yes, Doctor." She drained her glass and left him alone.

Dinner was a simple affair of lamb roasted on the fire. Exhausted after an eventful day, Lizzie retired to bed when the sun went down and fell asleep almost immediately.

The following day, she felt glad of the divided skirt as she picked her way across the uneven ground, following Quintillus. She worked on cleaning and cataloguing the previous day's finds, marveling at the workmanship on the shards of pottery and a perfect little alabaster statuette of the goddess Sekhmet. For something so small, it was remarkably heavy. Once cleaned, the green tint to the otherwise white alabaster gave the object a translucent quality. She turned it over in her hand. It felt pleasantly, but surprisingly, cold to the touch. She made to put it down and gave a little gasp.

She could swear it had moved by itself in her hand.

―――――

Over the next three days, Lizzie worked diligently, ensuring she packed every item carefully and securely. She saw little of Dr. Quintillus. He would appear at mealtimes but spent most of his time with Dressler.

On the seventh day, Lizzie awoke bathed in sweat, her head pounding and her stomach churning.

Abbas took one look at her and immediately fetched a bowl. Within seconds she was glad he had as she spewed bright yellow vomit into it. He handed her a glass of water, which she drank down. Her unquenchable thirst led her to drain a second glass. She shivered and her teeth chattered uncontrollably.

"You must lie back and rest, Miss Charters," he said. "I will inform Dr. Quintillus."

Lizzie sank gratefully down onto the pillow. When she opened her eyes again, Dr. Quintillus stood over her. Abbas pressed a cold, damp flannel against her burning forehead.

"I'm so sorry, Doctor. I…" Her mouth felt so dry, Lizzie could barely get the words out.

"You must return to the hotel. Abbas will accompany you and instruct them to summon a doctor."

"But the dig—"

Quintillus raised his hand. "I shall continue here and return to the hotel in a few days, when I trust you will be much recovered."

Lizzie felt too weak and sick to argue. She kept drifting in and out of consciousness and the camp bed provided precious little comfort. The thought of clean, cool, fresh sheets was seductive.

Barely aware of the journey back to Alexandria, strange images flashed into her fever-ridden brain, the alabaster statuette of Sekhmet coming to life and leaping at her. She cried out as wave after wave of delirium sucked her down. Through it all, the gentle voice of Abbas soothed her while the cool flannels he applied to her head eased the burning fever a little.

In her room, Abbas left her to get undressed as best she could. Lizzie felt relieved that everything had remained where she left it, so at least she didn't have to search around for a nightdress. As she lowered it over her head, the cotton cooled skin that felt as if an army of ants were crawling across it.

Lizzie tossed her clothes into the bottom of the wardrobe and, with a great effort, dragged the bedcovers back. Once in bed, with every muscle and nerve aching and throbbing, she lay back against the deep pillows.

The doctor prescribed quinine and complete rest, not that Lizzie could have done anything if she tried. Her legs buckled whenever she needed to go to the bathroom, and she could only walk by holding onto available pieces of furniture.

Abbas attended to her with care and compassion. Not once did she ever feel compromised by having a manservant rather than a lady's maid. He showed her total respect at all times, fed her soup when she felt she could hold it down, and brought her a bowl when she discovered she couldn't.

On the third night, she awoke to a flapping of wings directly above her head. She cried out in horror as a large white bird flew around the room. The door opened and Abbas dashed in, a bowl in his hand.

"Abbas, please get that bird out of my room."

He lit the lamp and shone it around. "There is no bird here."

Lizzie stared around incredulously. "It must have escaped through the door when you came in."

"Maybe..."

Lizzie could tell Abbas didn't believe it. She spotted a feather on the bed and picked it up. "Look, you can see I told you the truth. Where did this come from?"

Abbas picked it up and Lizzie remembered the white feather that had disappeared. But this one was gray. Like the white one, this feather was large, distinctively pointed, but it couldn't be the same bird. She said as much to Abbas as she told him of her previous experience.

"Caladrius," Abbas whispered.

"What? Caladrius? What's that?"

"It is a myth from long ago, Miss Charters. Caladrius was a large white bird that could take away sickness, but it paid for it. Its plumage would turn gray as it took on the illness."

Lizzie put her hand to her forehead, hardly daring to believe what she found. "My temperature's gone down."

Her headache had also gone, her muscles no longer protested at every movement and her skin had stopped feeling hypersensitive.

"Maybe Caladrius visited you. He took away your sickness and left a gray feather."

Lizzie settled back in bed, skeptical but bemused. "Whether that's true or not, I certainly feel much better. I think I'll sleep now."

Abbas left her and she slept soundly for the rest of the night.

The next day, although still quite weak, she got up, bathed, and dressed for the first time since returning from the dig. Two days later, she could not wait to return to Taposiris Magna.

"When may we leave, Abbas?"

"Dr. Quintillus told me he would return here after a week. He will then see how you are recovering."

"But I'm fine now."

"Then I am sure he will decide you are ready to return to the camp. You need patience. For a day or two longer only."

When Dr. Quintillus did return, he seemed encouraged by her appearance.

"I hear you have been an excellent patient, Miss Charters. I believe the doctor is satisfied with your recovery."

"He is indeed, and so am I. When shall we leave?"

"Tomorrow. Early. Eight o'clock."

At dinner that evening, Dr. Quintillus ordered them a bottle of chilled white burgundy, and it complemented the excellent Sole Veronique. Lizzie still needed to get her appetite back and ate sparingly — a fact not lost on Quintillus.

"You have become much thinner, Miss Charters. Are you sure you're ready to return to the camp?"

"I'm certain. Miss Bell has suffered much worse and still kept going. She has ridden through the desert for miles, irrespective of the conditions or her own comfort. I'm growing stronger every day, and I'm determined to return to full health as quickly as possible. Lying around here with nothing constructive to do will merely hinder that recovery."

"I admire your determination. It does you credit."

"Thank you, Doctor."

"I recommend you retire early this evening and get a good sleep to prepare for tomorrow. Remember, we leave at eight."

After dinner, Lizzie took the elevator to her floor and emerged from it. She swayed and grabbed the wall to steady herself. Her vision blurred, and the corridor shimmered in front of her. She could move, placing one foot in front of the other, but her legs wouldn't respond to her commands. It seemed as if someone outside her body had taken control. It didn't make any sense, but she felt as if she were a stranger inside her own body. Maybe the wine had affected her more than she thought one small glass could? Whatever the cause, she wished it would stop. Now. Her right hand removed the room key from her purse and inserted it in the lock. It opened the door, removed the key, closed the door behind her and locked it, while she watched the whole proceedings like a bystander.

Ten minutes later, her body took itself to bed, lying under the coverlet and closing her eyes. The strangeness continued into her subconscious as she drifted off to sleep.

———

A statue stood in front of her, in the shape of a large black cat. Its ears were pricked and it wore a magnificent jeweled collar. As she watched, the statue lost its sheen and became softer. It flexed its paws and its body became covered in gleaming fur. Its eyes shone like amethysts as it fixed her with a powerful stare. The sight mesmerized Lizzie so much she couldn't move. The creature began to circle around in front of her, its tail waving. Its head grew, the snout becoming more like a lioness than a cat. It opened its mouth to reveal large incisors and spat at her.

Lizzie understood the warning. She tried to back off, but her feet would not obey her and she remained rigid. The creature gave one last warning hiss, arched its back, and leaped at her. She fell downward into an endless black abyss.

Lizzie awoke, panting, disoriented. Surely the fever couldn't be returning. She put her hand to her damp forehead and swung her legs off the bed. At least her body seemed to belong to her once more.

In the bathroom, Lizzie looked at her flushed face in the mirror and ran the cold tap. She squeezed a facecloth almost dry and patted her burning cheeks. Her wrist stung and she winced. She glanced down and saw why. A three- or four-inch-long scrape. Bright red. A scratch exactly like that of a cat.

She hurried back into the bedroom and over to her bed where, on the sheets, she saw a few tiny droplets of blood.

And some black cat hairs.

The next day, Lizzie awoke late after sleeping so heavily. Her head felt full of cotton wool. She peered at her bedside clock. Five minutes to eight. She threw back the covers and prayed Quintillus would wait. She dressed hurriedly and readied herself to leave when she spotted a note pushed under her door.

Lizzie picked it up and unfolded the paper.

Dear Miss Charters,

As you are clearly still not fully recovered, I deem it wise to delay your return to camp. Please ensure you rest today. It was signed, E. Quintillus.

Lizzie cursed herself. How could she oversleep when she had promised him she had recovered? Why hadn't Abbas come to wake her? He must have returned to the camp with the doctor. So she had been left all alone. She had let Dr. Quintillus down. Lizzie railed at herself for her stupidity. Part of her felt tempted to simply go after him. After all, the hotel could arrange transportation for her. She had almost decided to do it when a voice inside her warned against it. He had *ordered* her to stay and rest. What sort of reaction would she get if she ignored his instruction and turned up there anyway?

Lizzie sighed and went down to breakfast. A long day stretched in front of her, with no plans how to spend it. After some deliberation, she decided to explore the grounds, and took care to stay in the shade of the palm trees that lined the walkways.

The hotel gardens boasted flowers of every exotic color. Vivid reds, blues, and oranges, and delicate scents she was unused to. Lizzie had never been a gardener and couldn't have begun to name the various plants, but that didn't stop her from appreciating the dazzling array. She found a bench and sat down with a book she had found in the hotel lounge. As soon as she started to read H. Rider Haggard's *The Yellow God*, a shadow passed in front of her and she looked up. A man dressed smartly in a gray suit smiled down at her.

"Forgive me, but my name is Hermann Ziegler. I am from the Lorenz Museum in Berlin." He bowed and kissed the back of her proffered hand.

"A pleasure to meet you, Herr Ziegler. My name is Elizabeth Charters."

"I already knew that Miss Charters. I wonder if you would permit me to join you for a few minutes. I need to talk to you about Dr. Quintillus."

Curiosity tinged with suspicion meant Lizzie couldn't refuse. She indicated a chair opposite her and he sat.

"I am most sorry for disturbing your morning in this manner, but when I saw you with Dr. Quintillus yesterday, I felt I had to speak to you. To warn you. I know you are personally acquainted with the doctor. I am afraid he has something of a record of influencing impressionable and vulnerable young women."

Something about his tone raised Lizzie's hackles. "Herr Ziegler, I am *academically* acquainted with Dr. Quintillus. I attend his lectures on ancient Egyptian history at the University of Oxford in England. Ours is a purely professional relationship."

"I would not presume to suggest any other, Miss Charters. Indeed, I would be most surprised if he had entered into a personal relationship with you, or with anyone, for that matter."

This took Lizzie by surprise. "What are you suggesting, Herr Ziegler?"

"I think you must know of the doctor's feelings for Cleopatra? His unnatural obsession with her is the talk of Berlin's academic circles — and elsewhere. His ideas are…unorthodox, shall we say. His methods even more so."

"I'm sorry, I don't know what you're talking about. I know of his keen interest in Cleopatra, of course. But he is an archeologist engaged in digging for artifacts, which I believe your museum has benefitted from in the past. I am here as his assistant. That is all."

"I wish it were so, Miss Charters. Truly I do. Unfortunately, I must tell you that such is not the case. It never is with that man. Over the years, he has traveled from Budapest to Leipzig, Paris, Madrid, Berlin, Oxford, Vienna. Where next, I wonder? He seems not to stay anywhere for more than a handful of years. Do you know anything about his history or his personal life?"

"Of course not. It's not my place to question him about such matters."

"He won't tell you anything even if you decide to make it your business. Plenty have tried. And regretted it. If he were here today, we wouldn't be having this conversation because I would be too fearful of the consequences to myself."

First her mother and Uncle Andrew, and now a complete stranger. Everyone seemed intent on besmirching Dr. Quintillus's character. "Herr Ziegler, please. I must ask to you stop this. He's a brilliant man."

Herr Ziegler shook his head. "I will not deny it. His is a brilliance. Of a kind. But I have great personal reason for my concern — and pity for anyone unfortunate enough to venture within his sphere."

"I can assure you I don't require any pity. Quite the reverse."

"Miss Charters, you are aware he intends to reincarnate Cleopatra, aren't you?"

That was too much. "Don't be absurd."

"Absurd? Really? I don't think so, and I am far from alone in that view. Did you know he found an ancient scroll tucked away somewhere deep in the archives of your university? It tells of the circumstances of Cleopatra's death and much more. There are those of us who believe he has stumbled on the actual location of her tomb and how to revive her."

"But that's preposterous. Revive a mummy?" It would be laughable if the man hadn't ventured so close to the truth. After all, the doctor had told her he had found a scroll and it had led him to Taposiris Magna. But, as for the rest…

"Have you ever tried to revive a corpse, Herr Ziegler?"

"Indeed not. It would never occur to me to want to commit such an immoral and blasphemous act."

"Quite apart from the fact that it goes against all the laws of nature and of God."

"As you say. Surely, by now, you know that to Quintillus, laws of God and nature don't apply. At least in his mind."

"I know nothing of the sort. I don't know what intention you had in approaching me, but I would appreciate it if you didn't trouble me again." Lizzie stood and hurried away, back to the peace and quiet of her room.

She spent the rest of the morning on her balcony overlooking the blue waters of the Mediterranean.

Quintillus returned a little after four in the afternoon. Lizzie had taken a short nap after lunch and heard his door swing shut.

She got up and rearranged her hair. Satisfied with her appearance, she went out and knocked on his door.

He answered it straightaway. "Ah, Miss Charters. I trust you are recovered now."

"I am so sorry I overslept. It's something I never do."

"No apology necessary. You have been ill and your body needs time to recover. I hope you spent a peaceful day?"

"Mostly."

"Mostly?"

"Yes. I…" A middle-aged woman passed them in the corridor and shot Lizzie a disapproving glance. "I wonder if we could go down to the lounge. I need to tell you about something odd that happened this morning."

Quintillus listened in silence, but with growing anger, judging by his expression. When she had finished her halting account of her meeting with Herr Ziegler, he spoke.

"I am acquainted with that man. He has attempted to thwart my every move. I trust you did not grant any credence to his words."

"No indeed, Doctor. I thought I should tell you what he said because it's outrageous that he should be slandering you in this manner."

Dr. Quintillus waved his hand. "It is of no consequence. Ziegler is a jealous man. He has achieved nothing in his own miserable life and sees no reason why anyone else should, either. I had no idea he was staying in this hotel, but I'm very glad you sent him off. I appreciate your loyalty to me. Think no more about it."

The following day, Dr. Quintillus allowed a delighted Lizzie to return to the dig. The heat still bothered her, but the sight of a small statuette of Isis she uncovered that morning more than made up for it. The doctor seemed pleased with her progress. Over the next few days, she managed to unearth shards of pottery from the Ptolemaic era and even some jewelry, among which was a gold and lapis lazuli oval brooch, decorated with the representation of a queen. Possibly even Cleopatra herself. The figure had been created in profile and demonstrated a noticeably prominent nose. If it should prove to be the queen, she certainly hadn't been the classical beauty legend had painted her.

One afternoon, having returned from the dig with Dr. Quintillus for a couple of days' rest, Lizzie witnessed an altercation at the concierge's desk. A tall woman in an elegant, broad-brimmed hat engaged in a heated argument with a well-dressed man Lizzie knew to be the hotel manager. She spoke English with a heavy German accent.

"I tell you my husband did *not* check out. He is still *here*."

The manager spoke as if placating a recalcitrant child. "Once again, I assure you Herr Ziegler checked out three days ago. He settled his bill. I have our copy of the receipt right here." The manager thrust a piece of paper into the woman's hands. At the mention of the name

Ziegler, Lizzie decided to hang around, remaining as inconspicuous as possible.

The woman studied the receipt. "I can see *someone* has paid it, in cash, but that could not be my husband. He never carries so much money around with him. Especially in Egypt."

The hotel manager clearly didn't appreciate the slur on his fellow countrymen. His lip curled. "Madame, I wish I could help you further but, as you can see, the gentleman is no longer our guest. Maybe he has moved to a different hotel."

"Show me his room."

"I beg your pardon?"

"I demand to see the room he stayed in."

"I'm afraid that won't be possible. Another guest is checked in there now."

"Either you show me his room or I will inform the police."

"Then that is what you will have to do, because I will not disturb my guest."

The woman stamped her foot hard. "You have not heard the last from me," she said, and stomped out of the hotel.

Lizzie sidled up to the desk. "I'm sorry, I couldn't help overhearing."

The manager looked wearily at her. "Yes, Miss?"

"The lady who was just here. Frau Ziegler. You said her husband checked out three days ago?"

"That is correct, Miss."

"Did you personally see him settle his bill?"

"No, Miss."

The concierge hovered nearby. Lizzie addressed him.

"Perhaps you served him?"

The young man shook his head. "I believe it was my colleague. It was my day off then."

"And is your colleague on duty now?"

"He has been away. Sick. He has a fever."

"Thank you." Lizzie moved away. A sense of trepidation niggled at her. For the life of her, she didn't know why.

Dr. Quintillus had taken to having his meals in his room so, after dining alone, Lizzie decided on a stroll before turning in for the night.

A full moon lit up the gardens, night jasmine scenting her progress. Not a soul passed her as she made her way along the path. In the distance, waves broke against the shore. The leaves barely rustled in the still air. She went farther than she had ventured previously and came upon a flight of stone steps. In the murky gloom, she could just make out that they would take her down onto the beach. The sky looked clear enough so she would have the moon to light her way.

She held onto the handrail and slowly made her descent. In the soft sand, she sank below the level of her low-heeled shoes. With some difficulty, she trudged along the beach, keeping to the cliffs.

She came upon a cave and peered in but found it difficult to make out anything in the dark and eerie gloom. She was about to move off when she heard a cry.

A man in obvious distress. In the cave.

"Hello?" Her voice echoed off the stone.

The cries were unintelligible. Whimpering and sobbing from someone in extreme pain. Lizzie strained her eyes but still could make out nothing. She took a few hesitant steps, and her right foot knocked against something hard and metallic. She bent down and felt around. Her hand brushed against a long, cylindrical object, which she picked it up. She held it out of the cave entrance, and the moonlight revealed a flashlight. She switched it on and mercifully the bulb worked.

She lost no time and shone the beam on the ground and around the walls. Then she saw him.

The man was hanging on the wall, suspended by his hands. As she approached, she gagged. Someone had driven spikes through his palms and pinned him to a large wooden board. Streams of dried blood stained his arms, and his chest was a bloodied mess. His shirt and trousers hung in tatters. On the ground lay a vicious-looking whip, with small spikes that had been used to virtually flay the man alive.

The stench of feces and urine assailed her nose and she gagged again. The man's agonized eyes stared out at her from a face swollen, bloody and bruised.

"My God, who did this to you?"

He struggled to speak, his lips cracked and bleeding. "Qui...Quin...till...us." His head lolled and, as she brought the flashlight closer, she recognized him.

"Herr Ziegler? It's Miss Charters, Herr Ziegler. I'm going to fetch help."

Lizzie scrambled out of the cave and along the beach to the steps. Back in the hotel, she hurried to the concierge's desk. The man looked startled at her disheveled appearance. "There's a man," she said, panting. "Someone has tortured him and he's in a cave on the beach."

"I fetch the manager."

"Yes, but hurry. There may not be much time."

A few minutes later, the manager and two members of staff followed Lizzie into the cave. They all carried flashlights and, with the enhanced illumination, Lizzie could see the horror that was Hermann Ziegler all too clearly. The hotel staff gasped, and one of them retched.

He hung exactly as she had left him, his head lolled to one side, his hands bearing the strain of his body. His feet were bare, and filthy like the rest of him, and his legs bent unnaturally. Battered and broken, no doubt. He appeared unconscious—or worse.

The manager hesitantly touched Ziegler's neck, feeling for a pulse. The spikes had dragged farther, tearing his hands so that more blood had flowed and was congealing.

The manager withdrew his hand and shook his head. He spoke in rapid Arabic to one of his colleagues, who dashed off.

"I am sorry. This man is dead." The manager lowered his head.

Lizzie covered her mouth with her hand, then removed it. "That was Herr Ziegler. The man who disappeared."

The manager looked up, startled. He glanced again at the tortured man. "I would never have recognized him. Who could have done such a thing?"

Lizzie refrained from telling him what Ziegler had said. The *last* thing Ziegler had said.

"The police will be here soon. I have sent the boy for them. I think we must wait until they arrive."

"Of course," Lizzie said. Now what should she do? Tell the police and risk Quintillus being arrested? Or keep quiet? But what if—God forbid—Quintillus had committed this terrible crime? Unthinkable, of course. What reason could he have to do this to Ziegler? Preposterous idea. Ziegler was jealous of him. The doctor had told her so. But what if…

Her mind still raced in turmoil when three police officers and—judging by the bag he carried—a doctor hurried into the cave. They had brought more flashlights. The senior officer spoke to the manager in Arabic and, by the way they kept glancing at her, Lizzie knew she had become the topic of conversation. Any second now and she would have to give her account of what she had seen. The doctor checked for a pulse and found none. A brilliant flash of light bounced off the walls of the cave as a policeman with a camera proceeded to take shots of the body and murder scene.

The manager spoke to Lizzie. "The police would like you to attend the station tomorrow morning at nine. They will take a statement from you at that time and request that you do not leave the hotel before then."

"Of course. I understand."

"They have asked that I accompany you, as they need a statement from me, too. Such a terrible business. He could have hung there for weeks, months, maybe even years. No one usually comes down to this end of the beach."

"I went out for a walk and, quite by chance, decided to go this way."

"Fate perhaps."

Lizzie didn't answer.

She knew Dr. Quintillus was due to attend a meeting with an official representative from the Egyptian Antiquities department the following morning. As usual, he stayed in his room and she didn't see him for the rest of the evening. That was probably just as well. It would have been awkward facing him after what had happened. The next morning, though, she had no option but to knock on his door. She had planned to accompany him back to the dig later in the day, and now wouldn't be able to. Lizzie braced herself when she heard the key turn in the lock.

Dr. Quintillus had dressed and looked ready to begin the day. "Miss Charters."

Lizzie took a deep breath. Now she had come face-to-face with him, her words tumbled out in an unexpected rush. "I found a body. Last night. Herr Ziegler. He'd been tortured and left to die in a cave on the beach."

Dr. Quintillus's expression gave nothing away. He merely nodded. "That must have been most traumatic for you."

"Yes. It was. I have to go to the police station this morning and give a statement so, I'm really sorry, I won't be able to go to the dig today." How inane she sounded.

"Of course. I quite understand. Good day, Miss Charters."

She faced the closed door, not knowing what to make of his reaction. Or lack of it.

At the station, she gave her statement to the senior police officer she had seen the previous night.

"You say the victim spoke just before he fell unconscious. What did he say?"

Lizzie's mouth ran dry. "He was mainly incoherent. Delirious, I suppose, with all the pain. He mostly cried out. No words as such until I asked him who had done this to him…" Her voice faltered. There would be no going back now.

"What did he say?"

Lying had never come easily to Lizzie. She could tell from the police officer's expression that he knew she wasn't telling him something.

He fingered the gun he carried in its holster. "I should warn you, Miss Charters. If you do not tell me some information that will assist us, I shall take a most serious view. What did he say? Clearly, he said something to you before he died."

Lizzie squirmed. "He was incoherent. In so much pain… Nothing he said made any sense. He had approached me a few days earlier and…"

"Yes, Miss Charters? And what?"

Lizzie shook her head. She was trapped. If she continued to say nothing she could end up in prison. And God alone knew what an Egyptian prison was like or whether they would ever let her out. If she lied, this man would know. She was certain of it. Surely, if Quintillus was innocent, he would be able to prove it.

"My patience is not without end, Miss Charters."

Lizzie licked dry lips. "He made contact with me because he also knew Dr. Quintillus, the archeologist. That was our connection. He saw me and said the one thing we had in common."

"Yes? What was that? Come now, you are doing yourself no good at all. I can tell you are trying to protect someone, and it will not work. Now, for the last time, what did he say? Was it a name?"

Lizzie nodded.

"And that name was?"

Forgive me. "Quintillus."

"This would be Dr. Emeryk Quintillus, also staying at the hotel?"

Lizzie's reply was barely audible. "Yes."

"You say you are also acquainted with this man?"

"Yes. I am here as his assistant on the dig."

The policeman made hurried notes. He said nothing. Lizzie sat with her hands in her lap and her heart thumping. What had she done?

When he had finished transcribing, the police officer read out her statement, translating from his own Arabic. Agreeing it sounded accurate, she signed it.

"Thank you, Miss Charters. You have been most helpful."

"What will happen now? Are you going to interview Dr. Quintillus?"

"Leave this case with us, Miss Charters."

She had been dismissed. Now she must face Dr. Quintillus.

Chapter 10

The doctor didn't leave for the dig as planned. Lizzie heard him return to his room in the late afternoon. Had he also been interviewed by the police? She kept expecting a knock on her door and a furious Dr. Quintillus demanding to know what she had done.

In the end, the stress of the previous twenty-four hours took its toll and she retired early, but every time she closed her eyes, she saw Ziegler hanging from that board, the cruel spikes tearing his hands apart. Why had he mentioned Quintillus's name if not to reveal his murderer? Although she had heard it with her own ears, Lizzie fought to find an alternative explanation, but even she had to admit the evidence was damning.

Eventually exhaustion took over and she fell into a deep and troubled sleep. Her dreams swirled in billowing mists, then cleared. Her door opened, although she knew she had locked it. She shrank back, clutching the sheets. The familiar tall figure entered. He stood by her bed, his eyes blazing.

"You betrayed me."

"I'm sorry. I had no choice. Herr Ziegler said your name…"

"Ziegler was a fool. He sought to undermine me. He intended to report me to the Egyptian authorities and have my dig shut down when I am about to make the greatest find the world has seen. I had such great hopes for you, Miss Charters. But now you have shown your disloyalty, I shall never be able to trust you again."

"I'm sorry, Doctor." For the first time since she had met him Lizzie felt real, tangible fear of what this man could be capable. "What will you do?"

Dr. Quintillus took out a cheroot from his cigar case and lit it. He took a deep drag and blew out a cloud of smoke. "Nothing. This does not concern me. They have no evidence I was anywhere near the man when the crime was committed. The only thing they have to go on is your statement. The word of a woman counts for precious little when compared to that of a person of standing such as myself. The case will remain open."

Lizzie blinked hard. In Britain he would never have got off so lightly. There would have been an investigation at least. She wondered briefly if he had bribed the police but, if he had, he was right. No one would listen to her. Suddenly, she wanted very much to return to England.

Quintillus stubbed out his cheroot. "As for you, Miss Charters, you will remain here and not leave the hotel for any reason until I say you may do so. Do I make myself clear?"

"It was not a betrayal, Doctor. I would never do that."

"Nevertheless, you told them my name."

"Only under duress." Could she feel any worse about herself? She had never seen him like this. So cold. Hostile. And it was all her fault. But somewhere, in the deep recesses of her mind, doubt was growing and with it, fear.

Quintillus made a dismissive gesture with his hand. "It will only be a matter of days now and then all that I have dreamed of will come true. You will not interfere with my plans any further."

He turned and left the room. Lizzie sprang out of bed and turned the key.

She awoke suddenly certain she had dreamed the whole encounter. The room was in semi-darkness. She sat up and peered at the clock on her bedside table. A little after five. She plumped the pillow and made to lie down again when something caught her eye. The ashtray. In it, a stubbed-out cheroot.

Lizzie slept no more that night.

She dragged herself out of bed at eight the next morning. Dr. Quintillus's nocturnal visit had been deeply disturbing. She knew he hadn't finished with her yet. That experiment he kept talking of. Presumably he still needed her help with it. He didn't give the impression of being a man to abandon his plans, especially where they concerned Cleopatra.

Lizzie spent her days trying to read books she found in the hotel's library, but concentration came hard and the words swam in front of her eyes. She walked in the grounds—although never down to the beach—and sipped tea in the sun lounge. Nobody bothered her and she saw nothing of any police investigation. It was almost as if the murder hadn't happened. She wondered if anyone had informed Frau Ziegler but, although she read the English language newspapers every day, she had seen no mention of his death. Peculiar to say the least, but maybe they did things differently here in Egypt? Whatever the answer, it had become clear she would get nowhere by pursuing it.

Finally, on the evening of July 19th, she saw Dr. Quintillus for the first time in over a week. His coat appeared dusty from riding but he had a look of sheer euphoria on his face as he advanced toward her in the lounge, his earlier anger with her apparently gone. Swept away by personal triumph.

"It is done," he said. "I have seen her. I have looked into the face of the queen and now she is safe forever."

"Congratulations, Doctor," Lizzie said cautiously. "How is she safe forever?"

"The tomb has been resealed and buried. It will not be found for many years. If ever. *He* was not with her—the Roman upstart who dared to think of her as merely his equal."

"Mark Antony."

Dr. Quintillus's lip curled. "I have work to do, and you shall assist me. Tomorrow morning we will meet here at nine."

He left her alone. For the rest of the evening and long into the night, Lizzie wondered what he intended. While he had made no mention of his earlier anger with her, Lizzie couldn't suppress the strong feeling that he wouldn't forget—or forgive—easily. She would have to exercise great care in future.

By nine o'clock the next morning, the fierce July heat had already asserted itself. Lizzie dressed in a cotton outfit that she hoped would keep out the worst of the sun's rays. The doctor arrived, punctual as always, and led her through the gardens and down onto the beach. Lizzie felt a pang of apprehension as he took them along the same route that led to the fatal cave.

She could almost taste her relief when he strode straight past it and on for another hundred yards to a larger cave. He led her inside. This one had a mostly even floor covered in sand. At the far end, a giant slab lay on the ground.

"Sit down on that," he ordered.

Every instinct told Lizzie to refuse. Whatever he had in mind, she wanted no part of it. She stood still.

"I told you to sit down. Do it. Don't make me have to repeat myself."

If she had retained any lingering doubts of his guilt, they fled in that moment, when Lizzie realized the nature of this man. A wretched sense of betrayal and shame at her own naïveté tore at her insides.

Slowly, she lowered herself onto the slab and sat.

Quintillus reached into his pocket and retrieved some gray dust. He poured it into a goblet that lay near the stone. From his coat pocket he took a small silver hip flask and poured a healthy measure of golden liquid into the glass. He swirled it around and gave it to her.

"Drink this. All of it, in one mouthful."

"No, I won't do it." Lizzie's words slipped out before she realized what she intended to say. The slap he gave her made her ears ring.

"You would defy me? No, you won't."

He dragged her hair back until her scalp screamed in pain. He forced her mouth open. She tried to bite him, but he redoubled his efforts and she felt as if her jaw would break. Her mouth opened and filled with brandy and ash. He clamped her jaws closed and held them tightly. She had to swallow. The brandy burned her throat and the ash made her choke. He hit her again, the force of it enough to distort her vision and send spasms of pain tearing through her head. She kicked out hard, her feet sometimes finding their mark, but he seemed to have the strength of five men. In one swift move, he dragged her hands behind her back, nearly wrenching her shoulders from their sockets. He bound them so tightly that the rope cut into her wrists. She kicked out again and he threw her against the cave wall, where she sank to the ground. In her semiconscious state, she couldn't fight him off as he bound her ankles together with more coarse rope.

Angry tears ran down her cheeks.

"You can't do this. You won't get away with it. Untie me."

He laughed. "Untie you? When I have gone to so much trouble to bind you? No, Miss Charters, I think not. Besides, in a few minutes, it won't matter."

Lizzie stopped struggling for a moment. "What do you mean?"

"My experiment. It is about to begin."

Lizzie took in the blazing eyes and arrogant posture of the man, and knew she stared into the face of evil. How could she ever have been attracted to such a monster?

Quintillus moved back to the stone and extracted a small gold statuette from his pocket. He took a little more dust from the pouch in his pocket and sprinkled it at the feet of the figurine.

He began a chant that echoed off the walls, gradually rising to a crescendo. Lizzie's head pounded, her vision swirled, and shadowy images emerged from the dark corners of the cave. More voices joined his, though Lizzie couldn't see where they came from. Louder and louder. Screams rattled her eardrums. Something touched her. She squirmed away. Hands. Claws. Tugging at her clothes. Twisting in her hair. Nothing of any substance to be seen, yet so much pain from the stabbing, insect-like assaults. Then, out of the corner of her eye, she glimpsed a sea of small beetles. Scarabs. Hundreds of them, crawling over each other, crawling over her. She screamed. Quintillus laughed. Laughter echoed all around her. Wild. Manic. Like the hilarity of the insane.

Lizzie screamed again. The scarabs were everywhere. Crawling up her legs, reaching for her face. She must be covered in bites. They burrowed into her clothes. She felt them on her breasts. Sharp claws. Still Quintillus laughed. Still, his unholy choir echoed him.

A figure appeared as a gray mist, taking form. A man. But not a man. It stood on two legs, but its head looked like no animal Lizzie had ever seen. One moment it seemed like a strangely elongated jackal snout, the next more like an aardvark. Two tall ears stood erect on top of its head, and it carried an ankh in one hand and a strangely shaped staff in the other. As it manifested itself, it grew taller, until it towered over Lizzie—its eyes menacing her. She recognized the god of chaos, war and storms.

Set.

Lizzie's muscles locked as fear coursed through her body.

Quintillus stopped laughing. The "choir" died down. He began chanting again, in that archaic language which had to be that of ancient Egypt.

Lizzie's vision blurred. Her consciousness drifted. In the distance, a mummified body lay still upon a stone slab. The vision morphed and Lizzie saw her as she must have been—a magnificent woman, dressed in white from head to foot. On her head, the royal diadem. She lay sleeping. Not sleeping. Dead. Lizzie stared down at her now. Out of her body. Weightless yet able to stand. Unbound and free of her captor.

She stared down at the mesmerizing face.

Cleopatra opened her eyes.

Chapter 11

The vision misted, and once again the ancient, mummified body lay in front of her. Somehow it had moved closer. So close, she could have reached out and touched the bandaged limbs. Lizzie screamed, but no sound came out. The dark eyes blazed with anger so profound she could almost taste it. The queen slowly raised herself into a sitting position. Only her face showed signs of life. Her torso, arms, and legs remained bound with bandages, black and gray with age and embalming fluids. But that face. Its eyes, heavily rimmed with kohl, the skin, olive and smooth. High cheekbones and a slightly hooked nose gave her a unique, if not classical, beauty. Full, red, sensual lips—those of a woman who could have captivated any man she chose.

Her gaze locked onto Lizzie's eyes and held her in a trance. She lifted one arm with apparent ease, her fingers pointing toward the frightened young woman. Lizzie felt an irresistible force tugging at her, dragging her. Her back bent, her face inched closer to the queen's.

Cleopatra's eyes hypnotized her until all she could see was one magnificent iris. Deepest violet. Drawing her into itself. She fought to break away but the power was too strong. Somewhere nearby, she heard a man's laugh. It could only be Quintillus. This must be what he wanted. This, the experiment he intended her to be a part of. With all her strength, she fought back. Her formless body screamed in pain. Her mind filled with images of beasts and demons, scaly arms, legs, bodies. Over all the chaos, the god Set wielded his staff, threw back his head, and roared.

Lizzie emerged from unconsciousness. It took her a minute to realize where she lay. Then she remembered. The cave. Thankfully, the bonds which had held her so tightly were gone, and she willed her numb feet to bear her weight. No sign of Quintillus or of the statuette. The cave was entirely empty. She had no idea how long she had been there but, limping to the entrance, the bright sunlight made her blink and her eyes tear up.

She picked her way back along the beach, pausing briefly at the cave where Herr Ziegler had been killed. She hesitated, but didn't go in, and resumed her journey back to the hotel. All the while, she wondered. Had what she experienced been real? Whatever Dr. Quintillus had given her to drink must have drugged her, and she couldn't know what else might have happened while she lay there, tortured by impossible visions.

Back at the hotel, she made straight for her room. She opened her trunk and piled her things back into it. Anything she had left at camp would just have to stay there. Lizzie worked fast and was putting the key into her purse when a loud rapping sounded at her door.

Dr. Quintillus? But what could he do in broad daylight in a hotel corridor? As long as she didn't let him in. She took a deep breath and opened the door a crack, ready to slam it shut if need be. Abbas stood there, a serious expression on his face. She hesitated a moment and then let him in.

"Miss Charters, I am instructed to take you to Dr. Quintillus immediately." He couldn't miss seeing the trunk and the empty wardrobe with its open doors. He raised his eyebrows.

"As you can see, Abbas, I have decided to return to England immediately. I cannot remain here any longer."

"But Dr. Quintillus—"

"Dr. Quintillus is the reason I have to leave. If I stay, I'm certain something terrible is going to happen to me. If it hasn't already."

Abbas looked at her questioningly, but Lizzie wasn't prepared to debate with him. "Thank you for all you did for me during my illness, Abbas. I'm sorry to have to do this, but I must ask you to leave. Now."

Abbas sighed deeply. "I too am sad I have to do this, Miss Charters." She didn't see the blow coming. Everything went dark.

She was tossed and turned from side to side, and Lizzie's head throbbed. She struggled to open her eyes and pain shot through her head from the bright sunlight.

"Ah. Miss Charters. I trust you are not in too much discomfort."

Lizzie struggled to sit up and glared at Abbas, whose expression of concern doubled when he saw her face.

"Why did you do that? I thought we were friends."

"I hope we can still be, but Dr. Quintillus insisted, and you should know that when he orders, you obey."

"Where are you taking me? Taposiris Magna?"

Abbas shook his head. "No. Somewhere nearby, but not there. Not anymore. I am not permitted to tell you."

"What does he intend to do to me?"

"I am not so far in the doctor's confidence that he tells me such things."

"I believe he intends to kill me in order to bring Cleopatra back to life."

Abbas's eyes grew wide. "But that is impossible."

"Tell that to Dr. Quintillus. I'm sure he attempted something like it yesterday evening. I don't believe he succeeded then, so perhaps he believes it will work better wherever you're taking me."

"I do not know any of this," Abbas said.

The carriage sped over dusty roads. The sun beat down, its brightness dazzling. Lizzie tried to make herself as comfortable as possible. Right now, escape would be impossible. She must wait for the right moment. If that ever presented itself.

They turned off onto a narrow track with potholes so large, they sent the carriage lurching again from side to side. Tall palm trees and grasses swayed in the hot breeze and framed the path. After several minutes, they came to a halt outside a small, dazzlingly white, ruined temple.

"We are here," Abbas said, and helped her down from the carriage.

He led her toward the entrance, which was flanked by four enormous Grecian pillars. Taking her hand, he helped her up the worn steps and through into a courtyard.

Ahead of them, Quintillus stood, waiting in the area that would have been the temple's inner sanctum. He had prepared an altar. On it, the statuette of Set stood next to a small, covered bowl. A sharp dagger glinted in the sun and Lizzie hoped its purpose was purely ceremonial, but either way, determination had kicked in and she stood with her head held defiantly high. The time for weakness and naïve faith had well and truly passed. Now she faced Quintillus as he unwrapped and unrolled an ancient papyrus scroll, laid it on the altar, and secured it at each corner with stones.

A wave of apprehension threatened to crumble her newfound resolve, but Lizzie set her jaw. She would not give him the satisfaction of seeing her emotions. Abbas stood to one side, just out of her line of sight. She wondered what he made of all this. Surely he wouldn't stand aside and watch while Quintillus murdered her.

"You cannot escape your destiny," Quintillus said.

"And what is that?" She felt proud of the defiance in her voice.

"My queen will live again in you."

"No. You tried yesterday and failed."

He looked around. "Now we are here. In this temple dedicated to Isis."

"Then what is that statuette of Set doing here?" She caught sight of a familiar small alabaster figure. "And Sekhmet?"

"I shall call on the collective power of the gods."

Lizzie thought fast. Maybe she could outrun Quintillus. If she made it back to the carriage, surely the driver would help her, even if Abbas would not. Desperate thoughts, but her situation could hardly be more desperate.

Quintillus turned his back on her and began chanting. She saw her moment and took off at a speed she didn't know she was capable of. Abbas didn't follow her. Neither did Quintillus. She had made it maybe halfway when a strong force tugged her backward. She fought against it, pushing on, but her feet wouldn't move forward. The force dragged her back and nothing she did could stop it.

"You see?" Quintillus said. "I have the power of the gods on my side."

Lizzie fell, limp and exhausted, to the ground in front of him. Despite her best efforts, there seemed nothing more she could do. Abbas continued to stand silently, but he bowed his head. Waiting, it seemed, for the inevitable.

The invisible force dragged Lizzie to her feet, and Quintillus took her hand and led her to the altar. The harder she fought not to move, the more the energy pushed her. She staggered up the two steps and Quintillus spread his hands. In an instant, Lizzie lay on her back.

The sky darkened like a solar eclipse. A rushing wind hurtled toward them. The surrounding palm trees swayed and creaked. Lizzie tasted sand and salt. All the while, Quintillus chanted and her mind became confused. Disjointed.

More visions. The dead queen's face, her magnificent eyes, all swirled up to force themselves into her consciousness. She felt a wrench and realized she had once again left her body. Weightless, floating, staring down—not at herself—but at the dead Cleopatra.

This time, she felt lighter, freed from her fears. She saw Quintillus brandish the statuette of Set in one hand and Sekhmet in the other. From somewhere she heard the growl of a lioness and the roar of the god of chaos. Surely Isis should have been here, in her temple, but the goddess of love was nowhere to be seen.

The queen stood and pointed at Quintillus. He seemed to waver for an instant, then recovered. His chants grew louder and more insistent. The wind howled and rain cascaded down on the scene Lizzie could now only witness. Above it all, she floated, suspended between space and time. The queen looked ghostly, lacking the form she had worn the previous night. Lizzie peered down at her own body, inert, peaceful. An empty vessel.

Waiting.

Chapter 12

Professor Charters replaced the telephone receiver and leaned back in his chair. His study was peaceful, a haven from the hustle and bustle of the world. Yet, even in this tranquil corner of civilization, evil could penetrate. The telephone call troubled him more than he cared to admit. He had never heard Lizzie's mother in quite such a state. What had happened to the girl? When he had calmed her sufficiently to allow her to string a sentence together, Flora told him that Lizzie had called her when she first arrived in Egypt, then sent her a telegram informing her she was going to the dig and wouldn't be back for some days. But when two weeks had gone by with no word, Flora telephoned the hotel. They flatly denied all knowledge of her, leaving her mother with no idea where her daughter had gone. A sense of dread gripped the professor.

A sharp rap on his door announced the arrival of Michael Sullivan, who breezed in, pipe in hand and newly returned from the Cotswolds.

"Gracious, Charters, old man, you look like someone dumped the worries of the world on your shoulders. Whatever's happened?"

Charters brought him up to speed. Sullivan let out a long breath. "I don't think it takes too much imagination to conclude that something is very wrong here. A young girl out there in the desert with a man of questionable character… What were you thinking of, allowing her to go with him?"

"She left me very little choice. Lizzie has always been strong-willed, even as a small child. I couldn't stop her. Her mother couldn't stop her.

When Lizzie fixes an idea into her head, I doubt Jehovah himself could prevent her carrying it out."

"What will you do now?"

"I don't really see any option but to go out there and try and find her."

Sullivan nodded and puffed on his pipe. "Fancy some company, old man?"

Charters thanked every deity he could remember. "I would be most grateful if you would join me. I confess I don't relish the thought of encountering Quintillus over there on my own."

"Quite understandable. The man is unstable and unpredictable. I dare say the two of us are more than a match for him, though."

Charters wished he could feel as certain as his friend.

Charters and Sullivan arrived at the Hotel Regal Imperial in Alexandria, hot, dusty and somewhat disheveled after their journey. Traveling overland and then by steamer from Brindisi in southernmost Italy, they had saved themselves nearly a week on the alternate route taken by Lizzie and Quintillus. The journey was, however, far more exhausting, especially in July, with temperatures soaring into the nineties.

The concierge greeted them and they checked in.

"I wonder if you could tell me when my niece, Miss Elizabeth Charters, checked out," Charters said.

The man behind the desk frowned. "Miss Charters?" He shook his head. "I do not recognize the name. When did she stay with us?"

"She should be registered with you still, but she certainly stayed with you three weeks ago."

"One moment, please. I check the register." He flipped back some pages and ran his finger down the list of names. "No, I am sorry, I cannot help you. She is not here. Perhaps another hotel? The Regal? Majestic? Imperial? I am afraid some of our names are so similar."

Charters raised his eyebrows at Sullivan. To the concierge, he said, "No matter. Thank you."

They moved away from the desk.

"What do you make of that, old man?" Sullivan asked.

"I don't know yet. Let me think about it. I don't know about you, but I do my best thinking in the bath."

"A long hot bath. What a glorious thought." Sullivan clapped his hands and they made their way to the elevator.

Charters welcomed the soothing soak and comforting towels, which eased his aching muscles. Changing into a fresh cotton shirt and trousers, he felt clean and refreshed for the first time in a week or more. Down in the lounge, he met up with a similarly spruce Sullivan.

The two men ordered beers and eased back in comfortable armchairs.

"What's your plan?" Sullivan asked, setting down an already half-empty glass.

"When I've drunk this beer, I'm going to see the manager and get to the bottom of this. Lizzie definitely stayed here. Her mother was quite specific about it. I can only think she didn't make herself understood. Long distance telephone calls can be tricky. All that interference. Then, first thing in the morning, I'm going to the police to report Lizzie officially missing."

Sullivan nodded. "It's certainly an odd business, but you're probably right. She could have spoken to someone whose English wasn't terribly good."

Charters drained his glass. "I needed that."

Sullivan finished his beer. "Ready?"

The professor nodded.

The manager invited them into his office and shut the door. After they had seated themselves, he began. "What can I do for you gentlemen? I trust everything is to your liking?"

"The rooms are fine, thank you. We are here about a guest of yours. My niece, in fact. Miss Elizabeth Charters."

Not even a twitch. "I'm sorry, the name is not familiar to me."

"Perhaps if you check your records? I believe she checked in on or around July first and, as far as we know, she is still booked in, although she spent part of the time onsite at an archeological dig not too far from here."

"Excuse me one moment, gentlemen, I shall check the hotel register." He left them.

Sullivan lit his pipe, blowing out clouds of fragrant smoke. "Maybe now we'll get somewhere."

"He's hiding something."

"I didn't see any reaction. I suppose he can't be expected to remember every guest's name."

"Her mother told me Lizzie had met with the manager on at least one occasion. That was another reason she knew Lizzie had been staying here."

The door opened and the manager returned. He sat down before he spoke.

"Gentlemen, I have checked the register, going back to the third week in June. There is no record of a Miss Elizabeth Charters."

Charters stared at him. "What about Dr. Emeryk Quintillus? You surely have a record of him staying here. In fact, he should still be here as well."

"Dr. Quintillus was here but left two weeks ago. I believe he has returned to his home in Vienna."

"*Vienna?* He lives in Oxford in England."

The manager's expression didn't change. "Perhaps I am wrong, but I am sure he listed his address as Vienna, Austria. I can check for you, if you like."

"No. Not now. Maybe later." Charters was aware of Sullivan's eyes on him. He felt suddenly stifled, as if someone had turned up the temperature. He needed to get out of this office.

"Thank you for your time." He stood. Sullivan did so as well.

"I am only sorry I could not be of more assistance. May I wish you both a most pleasant stay."

Back in the lounge, Sullivan bought Charters another beer. "Something tells me our manager friend is not being entirely honest with us."

"Oh, he was lying all right. The question is, why? And what's all that about Quintillus having a home in Vienna? Did you know about that?"

Sullivan shook his head. "I suppose there's no reason why he shouldn't. It did cross my mind he might be Austrian, or Hungarian. Or do they call themselves Austro-Hungarians since they became a dual monarchy?"

Charters shrugged. "It seems wherever we turn, we find something else about this man we didn't know. He was supposed to stay here for the entire summer. At least. Now it seems he's gone swanning off to Austria without informing any of us of his whereabouts."

"In breach of his contract."

"Precisely."

"Maybe now you have the excuse you need to oust him."

"Would that I could. While you were away, I approached Sir Henry, but as soon as I mentioned Quintillus by name he told me he was tired of what he called the vendetta against 'such a gifted and pioneering archeologist.' The man has the provost in his pocket."

"He seems to make a habit of that."

"Sullivan, what if he has done something to my niece? If he has, how will I ever face her mother?"

Sullivan patted him on the back. "Try not to worry, there's a good chap. I'm certain she'll turn up. As you said, she's a feisty young woman. I'm sure she's very resourceful and sensible."

"I can only hope you're right. We'll see what the police say tomorrow."

At nine a.m., Sullivan and Charters arrived at the Alexandria police station and asked to see the captain. They were shown into his office, and a smartly uniformed officer welcomed them.

"I understand you are reporting a missing person. A Miss Elizabeth Charters?"

"My niece," said Charters. "She was staying at the Hotel Regal Imperial, although they deny all knowledge of her."

"Why would they do that?"

"I have no idea, but you can imagine how concerned that makes us."

"Of course. You have a photograph, I understand?"

Charters fished out one of the precious few photographs he had of her. This one showed her in typical studio pose, dressed in a lacy white gown and standing next to an elaborate flower arrangement.

"A most attractive young lady, Professor."

"She came here as assistant to the archeologist, Dr. Emeryk Quintillus." Did he imagine the sudden flash of the captain's eyes? He wondered if Sullivan had noted it. "You know him, I should imagine?"

"Only by reputation. He is successful at finding artifacts and tombs."

"Indeed. Are you aware of his whereabouts now?"

"Not at this time. I wasn't even aware he was in Egypt."

He was lying. Charters was sure of it.

After agreeing to alert his officers to look out for the missing girl, the captain bid his guests farewell. As they emerged into the bright sunlight, Sullivan spoke. "Lying through his teeth."

"That's what I thought. Has Quintillus bought everyone in this city?"

"It certainly looks like it, doesn't it? Whatever is he up to?"

Charters put his head in his hands. "I honestly don't know where to turn now."

Sullivan fell quiet for a moment. "Fancy a trip to Taposiris Magna?"

Charters thought, then said, "I don't suppose it could do any harm."

"Let's hire a carriage."

————

The two men barely spoke on the journey, each wrapped in his own thoughts and fears. Silence greeted their arrival at the site, except for a breeze whistling around the old ruins, blowing up sand and dust. The place looked deserted. No sign of any camp, or fire. No timbers, buckets or sledgehammers.

"I suppose we're in the right place," Sullivan said.

"Definitely. Look at it."

Both men surveyed the ruins in awe. "It certainly *looks* like a place a person of importance would want to be buried in," Sullivan said.

"Indeed. A number of tombs have been found, but not the one *he* is looking for."

"If he had found it, don't you think we'd know about it? He'd be bragging about it from the rooftops."

"Perhaps. Unless he found it expedient to keep the discovery quiet."

Charters shot him a look. "What sort of expedience?"

Sullivan sighed and stared down at his boots, dusty with sand. "If he wanted her all to himself. Cleopatra, I mean, not your niece."

A dark cloud passed over the sun, obscuring it. Heavy drops of rain fell on the two men.

"What the devil?" Charters looked up, rain splashing his eyes. "Not a cloud in the sky a couple of minutes ago. Now look."

Sullivan's attention had been drawn elsewhere. "No, Charters, *you* look. Over there." He pointed to a cave entrance the professor hadn't noticed when they first arrived. In the gloom, Charters could make out the shape of an animal. A large, black cat. It prowled back and forth. Then it opened its mouth and growled. Sharp incisors flashed brilliant white. It hissed at them before disappearing into the cave entrance.

"Come on. Don't ask me why, but we have to follow it." Charters was already off after the beast. Sullivan hurried after him.

The rain stopped as they reached the cave entrance. No sign of the cat.

Charters picked his way carefully over the stones and assorted rubble on the cave floor.

"We really need a torch," Sullivan said, his voice echoing. Fortunately, the entrance was wide enough to let in a fair amount of light, but it grew darker the more they penetrated the interior.

A shuffling in the distance. Charters put his finger to his lips and the two men froze, listening.

A flickering torch flame danced shadows on the wall as a figure appeared around a corner at the back of the cave.

"Good afternoon, gentlemen. What a pleasant surprise."

"Quintillus!" Charters exclaimed. "What are you doing here, and where is my niece?"

Quintillus didn't reply. With an infuriating lack of urgency, he secured the torch in a bracket attached to the cave wall, took out his cigar case, and lit a cheroot, letting the smoke drift out of his nostrils.

"In answer to your first question, I am here on official archeological business, and to your second, I have no idea what you are talking about."

Never had Charters wanted to hit a man more than at that moment. Sullivan sensed his fury and held him back.

"Leave this to me, Charters. Quintillus, we demand you take us to Miss Charters at once."

"That would be extremely difficult since I don't know where she is."

"Well, when did you last see her, man?" Charters was barely restraining himself.

"Two weeks...maybe more. She left."

"Left? To go where?"

Quintillus spread his hands wide. "I have no idea. It is really none of my concern where your niece's whims take her."

"None of your concern?" Charters shrugged off Sullivan's restraining arm and advanced toward Quintillus, his finger pointing threateningly at him. "If you have harmed one hair of that young woman's head..."

"I advise you not to come any closer. You may regret it."

Charters took a step closer. "Where is she? I know you're hiding something. Out with it, man!"

The blow to his stomach came from nowhere. Charters doubled over, winded and in agony.

"What have you done to him?" Sullivan demanded.

"Nothing he would not do to me, if I let him."

"He hasn't laid a finger on you. That attack was completely unprovoked."

"Attack? I saw no attack. I merely saw a man suddenly double over in apparent pain. Surely that is what you saw, too?"

"I didn't see you actually strike the blow, but if not you, then who?"

Quintillus did not reply. Charters gasped for breath.

"You'll pay for this, Quintillus," Sullivan said, his voice rising. "I'll have you out of that university and your name blackened forevermore."

"I hardly think that's likely," Quintillus said.

Sullivan made a strangled, gurgling noise and clutched his throat.

"Let him go," Charters said, finally recovered enough to speak. "Whatever force you're using. You're killing him."

Quintillus laughed. "I am doing nothing. He is doing it to himself."

Charters looked again and saw that Sullivan's own hands were strangling him. He tried to move but couldn't. Sullivan's face had turned beetroot red, his eyes bulging, tongue protruding.

"For pity's sake, Quintillus. Stop this."

Quintillus stood watching the struggling man. "He can stop any time he wishes."

"Don't be ridiculous. Do you think he'd be doing that if he could help it?"

Charters exerted every effort of his own will to free himself and help his friend. Sullivan had dropped to his knees. He collapsed. Charters lurched forward and fell next to his friend. He ignored the shards of pain that shot up his legs from the sudden impact with the stony ground.

"You've killed him."

"I doubt that. He is merely unconscious."

Something snapped inside Charters's head. All reason rushed out and sheer blind anger took control. He lunged at Quintillus, who stood his ground.

"Don't take another step," he said.

Charters took another step.

He didn't see the cat until it landed on top of him, felling him to the ground. Its massive jaws locked onto his neck. He felt teeth tearing through his flesh. Blood spurted from the punctured carotid arteries and darkness descended like a veil.

The last thing Charters heard was Sullivan calling his name.

Chapter 13

Lizzie's spirit slipped through space and time. She floated above a scene of carnage. Two men lay mutilated and dead on the floor of a cave—their wounds so great, she could not distinguish their features at first.

Tendons, sinew, gore, and shattered bone littered the ground around the ruined corpses. She willed herself to look past the blood-soaked sand around them.

Her soul wept as she recognized Uncle Andrew. His companion must have been a friend of his, she guessed from Oxford. They must have come looking for her and now…

The bodies lay alone, but not for long. She sensed another presence. And more than that, she had a sense of herself, but not as she once was. She felt a tug, and the unmistakable figure of Quintillus came around the corner. But not alone. With him came the woman on whom she had gazed in the temple of Isis. Her face as enigmatic as before, she wore a floor-length gown of the purest white silk. Her eyes had been exquisitely made up in classical Egyptian fashion, and no trace remained of the filthy, stinking bandages she had been swaddled in.

With a stab of regret, Lizzie realized he had done what he set out to do. He had reincarnated Cleopatra, but he had used *her* to do it. Somehow, he had squeezed her spirit out of her body and replaced it with Cleopatra's, transforming her features into the image of the queen herself. Now he had his heart's desire and Lizzie's soul would be left to wander.

She tried to scream out, but she had no voice. She tried to will herself back into her body, but it was as if a steel door had slammed shut. Impenetrable.

Yet she somehow remained attached to her body, and she wondered if Quintillus even knew of her presence. As long as her physical self remained, it seemed her spirit accompanied it.

She had no connection with the spirit that had taken possession of her body, but the woman's eyes betrayed a bitter resentment. How long before this manifested itself? So far, the queen hadn't spoken. Maybe she couldn't. Perhaps she didn't know how to speak through someone unfamiliar with her language.

She saw too how quickly the woman tired. Only a few steps and she had started staggering already. Quintillus put his arm around her to steady her in a tender, loving gesture. He caressed her smooth cheek but she pulled away.

"Time enough for that," he said. "We have all the time we need."

Another flash of anger in those exquisite eyes. This time, the queen opened her mouth, but all that emerged was a strange clicking sound — like the tapping of claws — before she closed it again.

Quintillus half carried the woman out to the carriage that was waiting to take Charters and Sullivan back to the hotel. Lizzie's spirit followed them. A rapid exchange of Arabic ensued. The driver shrugged and Quintillus pressed British currency into the man's hand. Of course, he had sent his own carriage away so that the two men wouldn't suspect his presence.

Over the next few days, Lizzie's spirit traveled with Quintillus and his increasingly reluctant and unstable queen, on board a steamer from Alexandria back to Brindisi and then by a succession of trains to Vienna. In all the time they traveled, the woman inhabiting Lizzie's body never spoke a word. Quintillus catered to her every need, except the most intimate. That she managed for herself, although she needed Quintillus to support her as she limped down the corridor.

Wherever she went, Lizzie inevitably followed. Not always immediately. She had lost track and could tell the passage of time only by the day turning into night. She was unaware of the temperature falling as they traveled farther north, although it obviously bothered the queen. Cleopatra shivered constantly and made that strange clicking noise.

On a stopover in Milan, Quintillus booked rooms in a hotel in a quiet district of the city. He treated his companion with reverence, never suggesting anything improper, and ensured she had the best room in the establishment. The first morning they stayed there, he left the woman resting and returned a couple of hours later, laden with bags from some of the most exclusive shops the city had to offer. He persuaded her not to use makeup, as her exotic appearance had begun to attract too much attention. In the beginning, he had provided her with a kohl pencil for her eyes, but now he took it away from her.

She responded by picking up a hand mirror and smashing it against the far wall, leaving a dent in the plaster. The clicking noise became much louder, angrier, and echoed round the room. The inability to speak seemed to cause her more frustration, and a small vase soon followed the mirror. Quintillus quickly put all other breakable objects out of reach on the top shelf of the wardrobe, which he locked, dropping the key in his pocket.

They took their meals in her room. Quintillus served her but she ate hardly anything. The food seemed to disgust her, although to Lizzie it looked delicious. Quintillus ate heartily and did his best to encourage her, but she would throw her fork on the floor and upended more than one plate of food.

Eventually, they arrived in Vienna and the house in the exclusive district of Hietzing. Lizzie marveled at its magnificence, to which the queen seemed indifferent. The elegant marble hallway, large library stacked with books and adorned with a sumptuous ceiling painting, room after room filled with treasures. If only Lizzie could have touched them, sat on the ornate chairs, drunk from the crystal wineglasses…but it was not to be. Another woman used her body for those purposes. But each day, little by little, something was changing.

It started with her movements. Her walk became a heavy limp and her hands became uncoordinated. She would pick up a glass to drink from it and spill the contents all over herself. Still unable to articulate, the *tick-tick-tick* sound she made became more and more agitated and aggressive.

Quintillus waited on her, feeding her meals as much as she would tolerate—precious little. Lizzie only saw one member of his household—the butler, a lean, sour-faced Englishman called Butters. She knew Quintillus employed a cook and there must be other servants to keep the house running smoothly, but she never saw them.

The queen continued to deteriorate. Quintillus became anxious. He spent hours in the library, looking up endless references in books of such antiquity, Lizzie could only guess at their age. He lit black candles, recited invocations to ancient deities and, all the while, his beloved queen languished on a sofa, her skin paler each day. *My skin*, Lizzie thought, with a rush of regret so strong, she saw a momentary flash in the tired eyes. The queen looked through her, but Lizzie felt certain she had become aware of her, maybe she even saw her.

One night, Quintillus prepared a small altar in the library where the queen lay on a sofa. He dimmed the lights, lit his customary black candles, and placed a small cauldron on the altar. It smoked, and he murmured an indecipherable chant while crumbling leaves into the murky depths. He added some fine gray powder, and the atmosphere grew heavy in the room. Shadows lengthened. A strange rippling in the space around her put Lizzie on edge. In the room below, a greenish glow pulsed and grew stronger. A shape formed, and within seconds, the distinctive figure of the god Set towered above Quintillus.

He raised his staff, and Quintillus bowed his head.

The queen opened her mouth and a large scarab crawled out, followed by another and another until hundreds were crawling over each other. They spilled out over the sofa and onto the floor where they scurried toward the blazing fire. By the dozens, they were absorbed by it. Their bodies crackled as their carapaces split in the heat of the flames.

"Oh my queen," Quintillus said, "I have failed you this time, but not again."

The queen sank back, exhausted. She closed her eyes, her pale lips cracked and dry.

The next morning, Lizzie sensed a more significant change. Not white anymore, the face of the woman looked gray. Her eyes had grown dull and lifeless, and she seemed in pain. She had spent the night on the sofa, refusing all efforts by Quintillus to help her up to her bed. With his help now, she struggled up but could barely stand. To her horror, Lizzie saw a spreading dark stain on the cushion beneath her. For the first time, the normally composed Quintillus flinched, while tears flowed down Cleopatra's cheeks.

"My queen," he said, recovering himself and holding her. She collapsed in his arms. The invisible thread that bound Lizzie's spirit to her body tugged at her. Her vision blurred and she found herself in Egypt once more, but not the Egypt she recognized. Here, the great temple of Taposiris Magna rose up from the desert, gleaming in the sunshine. Everywhere, men and women went about their daily business, dressed as she had only seen in classical wall paintings.

She heard snatches of conversation she couldn't understand. A part of her wanted to stay there, but another wrench and she hurtled back to the house in Hietzing, where she looked down at the unfolding scene.

Quintillus held the woman's hand as she lay on the bed, eyes closed. "Rest now, my beloved," he whispered and raised her hand to his lips. Lizzie could almost feel the featherlight touch of his lips on her skin.

Then she wasn't there. And she wasn't alone. She sensed another presence right next to her, and there stood Cleopatra, as she must have been in life. Tall, strong, powerful, a haughty expression on her striking face. She spoke and Lizzie could understand her.

"I will be avenged. He shall not live."

"But how?"

Cleopatra did not answer. Her eyes blazed. Lizzie felt, in that moment, a connection she hadn't experienced before in all this strange non-life she had been living. Their two souls met, and Lizzie understood. Cleopatra no more wanted this than she did. This was a woman used to being in control. No man would rule her. No man ever had. Her love for Mark Antony overrode all other considerations. Quintillus, in his selfish obsessiveness, had torn her away from the one she craved to be with for all time. She must return to him.

Lizzie's eyes dimmed. The vision faded until it was merely a speck of waning light, growing dimmer with each passing second.

Once again, she looked down at the body on the bed, and she knew the spirit that possessed it was slipping away. To go where, Lizzie did not know. Perhaps back to that tomb in Taposiris Magna. Perhaps to fly free.

Quintillus sobbed quietly. His grand experiment had failed. But somewhere deep within this house, another spirit had stirred. Lizzie could sense it moving around. Human, but not human. Another ancient soul perhaps? But she had no answer.

Gradually, the woman's features changed. The exotic look of the Egyptian queen faded, replaced with a face Lizzie knew all too well— her own. She felt herself slipping, being gently pulled back by the invisible life thread. For a second, she sensed an emptiness in the vessel she now entered. Then she could feel her arms, legs, terrible pain in her head and a crushing weight on her chest. She took her first gasping breath.

Her last gasping breath.

Her sight faded on a large white bird circling above her.

Chapter 14

The void opened to welcome her. Strangely peaceful. Cloaked in nothingness that somehow soothed her tortured spirit. Time lost all meaning. The only sound a gentle lilt, like sweet music played under water.

Freed from her body, released from the constraints of corporeal life, Lizzie gradually gave herself up to her new surroundings, that had neither shape nor form, and no substance except what she felt deep in her soul.

The world she had known went on without her. Battles were fought. Countries claimed short-lived victories before they went to war again. Leaders came and went. Babies were born, grew up, married, had their own children, and died. Two generations passed.

And one day, Lizzie woke up.

———

The shock of her first conscious breath overwhelmed her. She stood in the library of the house in Hietzing. It looked exactly as it had the last time she had seen it, but *she* didn't. A mirror nearby caught a reflection. In shock, Lizzie realized she was staring at herself. But nothing about her looked the same. Her hair was now long, thick and black, eyes brown, and her skin olive. And her clothes! White shirt, open at the neck under a black jacket. She looked down, shocked to see she wore slim-fitting matching trousers and shoes with a pointed toe and high, narrow heel.

"Fräulein Zimic?"

She turned to the source of the voice, without a clue how to respond. The man wore an unfamiliar style of dark blue suit with pale blue shirt and tie. His gray hair had been neatly trimmed and he had a distinguished air about him.

"Fräulein Zimic, are you quite well?"

Lizzie inhaled deeply, the long-abandoned practice new and strange to her. Only one thing for it. For now, she would have to play along with this charade until she could understand what had happened to her.

Her voice sounded deeper. A stranger's voice in a stranger's body. Where had its owner gone? What had happened to Fräulein Zimic?

"Perfectly," she replied, and realized she had just spoken in German. But, of course, the man was speaking German, too.

"Is everything in order? Do you wish to proceed?"

"Proceed?" She tried to sound as natural as possible, but she could tell her change of attitude confused him.

"With the purchase of this house? You said a moment ago that it was exactly what you were looking for."

"Oh, the house. Yes, of course. How beautiful it is."

The man frowned. "Perhaps you would like a glass of water? Or some coffee?"

"No, no. I think I must be going now." Though where she would go was another matter.

"When will you decide?" The poor man looked as if he had stepped into another world. Appropriate, considering *she* certainly had.

"Oh, in a few days. I will get my affairs in order." That, at least, she could say with some honesty. When she could work out why she had come here and how long she was meant to stay.

"Very well." He didn't sound too pleased, and Lizzie had a hundred questions she wanted to ask him but daren't. This Zimic woman had been in the middle of agreeing to buy Quintillus's house and certainly wouldn't appreciate Lizzie wrecking things for her. The man showed her to the front door.

Out on the street, with the door shut firmly behind her, Lizzie experienced the shock of her life. Instead of horse-drawn carriages and the cars and buses she was used to, she discovered a world of gleaming metal and a rainbow assortment of colors. Red, yellow, white, silver, green…strangely shaped vehicles of every size and hue raced up and down the street.

Lizzie, in her new body, stared. Everywhere she looked, people were dressed as she was, or more casually, in clothes she had never dreamed could exist. Men and women with long hair, wearing identical blue, heavy-duty trousers. Difficult to tell which sex was which in some cases. Young women, her age, in skimpy shirts that clung to every curve. Others in skirts so short they barely protected their modesty. A tram rumbled by. At least *that* looked similar to others she had seen, if a little futuristic.

On the corner of the street, a box containing newspapers drew her attention. She peered down at the date. Thursday, June 2, 1977.

1977.

A sudden pain sent her reeling into the arms of a middle-aged woman. Speaking in rapid but soothing German, the woman led her to a nearby bench and Lizzie gratefully sank down. She assured her helper that she merely felt a little dizzy. The hot sun. She hadn't eaten. The woman left, after lecturing her on the need to maintain a regular diet.

Other passersby ignored the confused woman on the bench. The pain had subsided to a dull ache, but with it, Lizzie had to acknowledge an uncomfortable fact. She wasn't alone in this body. And its owner wanted it back.

Lizzie sat for an hour, trying to grow accustomed to the unfamiliar thoughts in her head. Knowledge of another person's life. Intimate details in some cases. She learned the body's first name was Gerda, she was thirty years old and from a family of wealthy industrialists who had grown rich during a war Lizzie knew nothing of. She discovered that Fräulein Zimic did indeed intend to buy Quintillus's house and that she could do so by paying cash.

Lizzie allowed herself to be steered by her host to a large, sleek, dark blue car with an insignia of a three-pointed figure within a circle and *240D* on the back.

Her hand automatically went to a pocket of her jacket and extracted some keys. She used one to unlock the driver's door and settled herself in the seat, momentarily baffled by the array of dials and levers in front of her. She may not have had the first idea of how to drive this strange machine, but Gerda Zimic did. Soon they were leaving the leafy suburbs behind and driving through countryside, baked in a hot sunny afternoon.

She stopped the car outside a large, rambling house, set in immaculately maintained gardens. An ornate, Grecian-style fountain stood in front of the entrance, the water gleaming like crystal as it poured over statues of gods and goddesses.

Lizzie mounted a sweeping stone staircase, unlocked a pair of sturdy wooden doors and entered a hall resplendent with yellow roses. A young woman asked her if she wanted a cold drink and Lizzie asked for lemonade. What she got as she sat in the lounge was a fizzy, clear concoction tasting vaguely of lemon and chemicals. She set it down after one mouthful.

She looked out over a rolling lawn, bordered by pine trees and brightened with an abundance of flowers. A large gray bird soared up into the sky. It looked out of place somehow, but surely she had seen it somewhere before? A fantastic, impossible creature.

An older woman her Gerda-self recognized as her mother came in and kissed her on the cheek. Through her, she learned that she should have signed the papers for the house that afternoon. Why had she come back so early? Lizzie improvised. She told her she didn't want to rush into it. She wanted one more night to sleep on it before committing fully.

Her mother seemed satisfied with that, emphasized what a bargain she had been offered and that she mustn't keep Count Markus von Dürnstein waiting or she would lose it. Now, at least, Lizzie knew who the distinguished-looking man had been.

———

After an evening spent acquainting herself with a father, brother, and sister, as well as the rather charming mother, Lizzie fell into bed and slept. When she awoke the next morning, it took a few moments to remind herself where she was and, more importantly, *who* she had become.

At breakfast, she found herself agreeing to her father sending their trusted butler to the Villa Dürnstein with the cash for the house purchase. Lizzie would follow on once she had eaten. She still felt curious as to why such a major purchase would be transacted in cash and wanted to ask but knew it would sound odd. The real Gerda would know the reason only too well.

Her father provided at least a clue. "Remember, Gerda, you don't answer any questions about this money. You assure the count that there is nothing illegal about it and that it is your preferred way of doing business. He wants to sell this property badly enough so I doubt he will ask too many questions."

Lizzie nodded and tucked into scrambled eggs. Questions tumbled in her mind and again she grew aware of Gerda's presence. A restless spirit, possessed of a certain arrogance and a determination to rid herself of Lizzie's presence, whatever she had to do to achieve it.

At the Villa Dürnstein, the house's current owner greeted Lizzie. He seemed far more relaxed than on the previous afternoon. Hardly surprising. Now many thousands of schillings richer, he had rid himself of a house he clearly detested for reasons Lizzie couldn't begin to fathom. She sensed relief as he patted the metal case containing the cash which had arrived, he said, half an hour earlier.

Lizzie noticed a leather suitcase in the hallway.

"You are leaving today? So soon?" she asked.

"I haven't lived here for a number of years. I just packed the last few mementos to take with me. Once you've signed the papers, the house is yours and you are free to move in whenever you like. Today, if you wish."

"Thank you," she replied.

He indicated a sheaf of typewritten sheets, laid out neatly on a polished wooden table. Next to them, a gold pen.

"If you would care to sign these," he said.

Lizzie nodded and sat at the table.

She quickly scanned the document. Once she signed it, this house would be hers. She reached the end and automatically signed her name.

Elizabeth Charters.

She stared at it in horror. Too late to do anything about it now. She could hardly cross that out and try to somehow summon Gerda to sign her own name.

With relief, she watched the count shove the documents in a briefcase without examining them. He handed her a set of keys, shook her hand and left.

Lizzie wandered from room to room, up and down the stairs. Apart from the library, the rest of the house had fallen into disrepair. Clearly, no one had lived in it for years. What furniture remained had been shrouded in white sheets. By contrast, a smart, modern kitchen had recently been fitted with all sorts of equipment Lizzie had never seen before and didn't have the slightest idea how to operate. It appeared neither did Gerda who, no doubt, had always been used to staff to do it all for her.

At the far end of the kitchen, a solid wooden door, double padlocked, seemed strangely out of place amid the stark white and gleaming steel of the rest of the room. Lizzie wandered up to it. There was no key in the lock or the two padlocks, which seemed a little excessive. She examined the keys Count Markus had given her, selected one and tried it in the door. It didn't work. She tried another, then another and finally, the lock sprang free. Two smaller keys fit the padlocks and she carefully lay each one down on the drainboard.

The door opened easily and, thankfully, the light switch worked.

In her spirit form, when attached to Cleopatra, she had never ventured into this part of the house. What use would an Egyptian queen have had for a basement? Lizzie made her way carefully down the dimly lit stairs. At the bottom, a corridor led to a much larger kitchen than the one upstairs. Here, she found an oil lamp and matches. With the light to guide her, she picked her way over the dusty floor. She shone the lamp over the walls. Copper pans, green with verdigris, hung from them. An old kitchen range, in dire need of black leading, stood cold and covered in dust and grime.

Lizzie moved onward, through the kitchen, past a wine store and butler's pantry, until she came to a dead end. A wall. It looked of fairly recent construction. The stillness grew heavy around her. Oppressive. She could almost taste it. Inside her, Gerda's trapped spirit stirred.

Lizzie felt her fear as it merged with her own. A coil of terror swept through her body. She had a powerful, overwhelming sense of something behind her. So close now, almost touching her. She daren't turn around.

She must turn around.

A chunk of plaster fell from the wall in front of her. Then another. And another. The plaster fell like snow. She stared at it. It stopped.

And then she turned around.

Lizzie recognized her instantly. The young woman was dressed as she was in the painting in the library. In her hand, she held a gleaming dagger. The figure shimmered, alternated between almost transparent and solid. Her stare mesmerized Lizzie.

Lizzie breathed her name. "Arsinoe."

The figure nodded, slowly. "You have come to me. And I have come for you."

"I don't understand."

"We need rebirth."

"We?"

"*I* need rebirth."

But she meant "we." Who was the other spirit? Only Arsinoe stood before her. Was there another, hiding in the shadows?

"You have brought the life force."

"Are you the one who trapped me in this woman's body?"

"I needed the life force. The woman you inhabit was buying this house. She was the obvious choice."

"You didn't need to kill my body. What possible purpose did that serve?"

"I did not kill you."

"Dr. Quintillus, then. He killed me when his experiment failed, but you were the one who put me into this body."

"It was necessary."

"But why do you need me? My spirit? You have hers. Gerda Zimic's."

"I will be avenged. My death at the hands of my sister must be paid for."

Now Lizzie understood. Because Quintillus had chosen *her* to be the vessel for Cleopatra's reincarnation, he had established a link—one which Arsinoe was determined to exploit for her own ends. But the experiment had failed. Cleopatra's spirit had been released to return to her body in her tomb and Lizzie had lost her own physical life in the process. Surely Arsinoe didn't mean to try again?

She seemed to read Lizzie's thoughts. "This time it will be done. Caladrius has brought you back. He has done my bidding."

Caladrius. So Lizzie had really seen it. Maybe Caladrius *had* cured her sickness in Egypt, as Abbas suggested. But this time was different. Now the bird had been pressed into service by this woman, whose intentions were pure evil.

Lizzie awoke, slumped in a comfortable chair in the library. She glanced up at the painting. There stood the girl, dagger in her hand. Strange she had never seen that before. She could have sworn she was holding back reeds.

Switching between her new life in this house and her host's old life became gradually less strange as the days became weeks and Lizzie settled in, with a butler, housekeeper, cook, and maids to renovate and keep her house immaculate. Gerda's mother insisted on bringing her camera and photographing the rooms, including the basement, so that she would have a lasting record of the improvements she had made. Her mother had the pictures developed and met up with her one morning for coffee at Lizzie's home.

Gerda's mother seemed agitated and on edge.

"It's really most extraordinary. I took all these myself so I know they weren't tampered with."

"I'm sorry. I don't follow," Lizzie said.

The older woman removed a large batch of photographs from a wallet. "All the pictures are fine, except for those I took in the basement. I needed to use the flash as it is so dismal down there and…well, see for yourself."

She lay four color photographs on the table. Lizzie picked them up, not daring to believe her eyes.

There were the familiar kitchen utensils, the scrubbed table, range, chairs, exactly as she knew them to be. But there was more. A ghostly figure of a man, with no eyes. He wore a stovepipe hat.

"Dr. Quintillus," Lizzie whispered.

"What did you say?"

Lizzie shook her head and handed the photos back. "Nothing. That's certainly peculiar. Maybe another photograph somehow got itself superimposed on those shots."

"If it did, I'm sure I would have remember taking a picture of that extraordinary-looking man." She shuddered. "Anyway, I showed them to your father. You know how interested he is in the supernatural. I've never understood it myself but there you are. He could have worse hobbies. He's all for sending them off to one of those haunted house magazines. Naturally I told him I thought the idea was quite absurd, but he's adamant. He wants to send them off in your name."

"What?"

"I know. Crazy. But you know your father, once he has an idea firmly fixed in his head, there's no shifting him. In the end, I agreed to ask you. I wouldn't normally entertain any such thing, but, as you know, he hasn't been feeling too well this past week or so and I think it might give him a boost. Finally, after years of searching, a ghost lands on his doorstep." She laughed.

"You don't really believe that, do you?"

"Of course not, but would you let him do this?"

Lizzie thought for a few moments. "Very well, if it means that much to him. Just as long as I don't get hordes of sightseers breaking down my door."

"Oh, I'm sure they don't reveal your actual address. It's the photographs they'll be interested in. I expect they don't believe in this stuff themselves. It's just an easy way to make money. Nevertheless..." She looked at one of the photos again. "I wish I did know what had created this odd effect. It must be a trick of the light or the flash, but it's so realistic."

After the woman had gone, Lizzie made her way down to the basement and into the deserted kitchen.

"Where are you hiding?" she said to the shadows. "I know you're here somewhere. I'm not scared of you anymore. What do you want of me?"

A tap dripped one solitary drop. It sounded loud in the suffocating stillness. Lizzie moved off, down toward the wall at the end of the corridor.

She could find no broken or chipped plaster to show what she had been sure she witnessed weeks earlier.

"I know you are here. Both of you."

The voice had lost none of its gravitas. "You are quite right, Miss Charters."

At first she couldn't see him. Then it seemed as if another set of eyelids opened and she could see him standing at her side. In profile.

As he turned toward her, she had her first sight of the dead Emeryk Quintillus. His skin seemed gray, dry, almost mummified, but his eyes unnerved her the most. Both sockets were empty. Two black holes remained. Yet, from his movements, he seemed to somehow be able to see.

"Now my house is restored to me, I no longer have any need of you. But Arsinoe does. It appears she needs you to let her into this woman's body, so she might live again."

"And what do her wishes matter to you? You used me to reincarnate Cleopatra and, when that didn't work, you condemned me to this half life, neither living nor dead, with no body of my own to return to."

"I do not possess Arsinoe's power. What she does with you is up to her. I will have what I desire, and, in return, she will be reborn."

A movement in the corner of her eye distracted her. Arsinoe.

She stood beside Quintillus and spoke. "I shall reclaim my life."

"And what will happen to me?" Lizzie felt she already knew the answer.

"I will set your spirit free."

"And Gerda Zimic?"

"She is the life force now. I need her in order to live."

"So she will be condemned to remain trapped in a body she no longer controls, until you decide you've had enough of her."

"She will age and all too soon will be unsuitable. Then I will have need of someone else. At that time, I shall do as I will for you. Set her spirit free to move across the desert and into the world beyond."

"And Quintillus. What does he get out of this?"

Arsinoe smiled. "My sister."

"But who… How?"

"That is not your concern."

From a distance, moving ever closer, Lizzie heard the rhythmic beating of huge wings.

Her voice echoed strangely, as if heard through water from a long distance away. Lizzie felt a tug. Like before. The invisible force dragged her out of Gerda's body. She didn't struggle but allowed herself to be pulled ever farther away. In a corner of her consciousness, she saw a huddled figure weeping. Gerda Zimic. Lizzie tried to reach out to her, but she had become all spirit. For a second, it seemed the woman became aware of her presence so close by. Her dark eyes looked up, as triumph replaced the sadness.

Released from Gerda's body, Lizzie floated free. The huge white bird steered her away from the body, the house, the world. A tunnel opened up and swallowed her. Her last thought was of the woman. Gerda Zimic. And then her consciousness left her.

Chapter 15

Gerda Zimic stretched her legs and sat up with a start. Such a strange dream. She looked around her. An old kitchen that obviously hadn't been used in years. She examined her hands in distaste. How had her nails grown so unkempt and chipped? And her fingers—so dirty from touching the filthy floor. She struggled to her feet, wishing the wooziness would leave her and she could stand up straight. What was she even doing down there in the bowels of this house? And where precisely was she?

Her mind refused to cooperate. An image of a young woman dressed in Edwardian clothes with clear hazel eyes and a fresh complexion drifted in and out of her brain. But Gerda didn't know anyone like that.

She must find out what had happened to her and get her bearings. Her limbs ached as she forced her unwilling legs to move. Slowly, she staggered through the kitchen, using the sink, table and wall to steady her as she passed along the corridor and finally arrived at a flight of stone stairs she couldn't remember descending.

What the hell is the matter with me? Did I get blind drunk? How long have I been here?

She grasped the handrail and half crawled up the stairs. At the top, she found herself on familiar territory. This was the house she intended to buy. The heavy door to the newer kitchen stood wide open—another mystery since it had been firmly locked the last time she could remember seeing it.

Her mouth felt so dry she could barely swallow. Gerda closed the door behind her and reached for a glass. She half filled it with cold water and drank it all down, realizing how thirsty she was. She drank another and finally began to feel a little stronger.

She crossed the hall with firmer steps than a few minutes earlier and went into the library.

The distinctive smell of lilies met her at the door. Glancing around, she could see no flower arrangement of any kind, but then some rooms had their own individual smell; maybe this was the library's version.

She went over to the window and gazed out over the garden. *Her* garden. She must have moved in already. Judging by the overgrown grass and weeds, she hadn't yet employed a gardener. That would need to be rectified. Tomorrow. She would ring the agency and they would send someone. That's what Mama always did. She wandered over to a small table on which stood a tray containing two decanters, one filled with cognac and one with scotch. A jug of water stood next to it as did a lead crystal tumbler. She selected the scotch, poured herself a generous measure, and topped it up with water.

The door opened and a maid appeared. Gerda didn't recognize her. How long had she lived here? The girl spoke.

"Will you be dining in this evening?"

Gerda hadn't a clue, but her grumbling stomach informed her she hadn't eaten in some time. "Yes." She would have to look for a tactful way of finding out the girl's name—and the rest of the staff, too. There had to be a cook. This girl was a housemaid. Besides, Mama always had a cook, butler and housemaids. Maybe she had even arranged for them all. It was the sort of thing her mother would do.

A name floated into her head. "Clara."

"Yes, Fräulein?"

"Thank you, Clara."

The girl nodded and left, closing the door quietly behind her.

Gerda sipped her drink and stared up at the seemingly endless bookcases, stuffed with all sorts of learned works. Maybe she should look at selling them. She would certainly never read them. The most Gerda read was *Vogue* and *Elle* and other glossy fashion magazines.

She caught sight of her hair in a mirror and gasped. Her fingers became tangled in the normally glossy waves. It felt like straw. Whatever had she been doing to herself? Maybe she had been ill. That would explain quite a lot. Except that the maid hadn't mentioned anything, which she surely would have if her mistress had been missing or sick.

Gerda switched on the TV. Maybe if she saw the news it would trigger something in her brain. On ORF1, the lunchtime news bulletin was just beginning. The date flashed up on the screen and Gerda did a double take.

September 3, 1980.

Three years. Three whole years had passed since she remembered anything.

Gerda poured herself another drink. The newsreader droned on. In the US, Ronald Reagan and Jimmy Carter launched their presidential campaigns. Reagan had made some misjudged comments about the Ku Klux Klan. Riots in Paris. Israeli Prime Minister Begin had agreed to resume talks with Egypt's President Sadat after the US elections in November…

It all floated over Gerda's head. She thought of calling her mother, telling her the awful three-year mental blank she was suffering. She even picked up the phone, but then put it down again. Her mother would worry. She would insist on Gerda seeing some expensive shrink. Above all, she must not panic. There would be a simple, logical explanation. All she had to do was find it.

When the news finished, she switched off the TV. The strain of the past hour had taken its toll—along with the scotch. Gerda took herself upstairs, intending to lie down, but a sudden draft at the foot of the stairs leading to the top floor made her keen to investigate.

She mounted the stairs and the draft became stronger. Maybe one of the servants had left a window open a little too wide. At the top, Gerda looked along at the bedroom doors. All except one were shut. She padded along the corridor to the open door and peered inside. The room was sparsely furnished with a single bed, covered in a worn and faded quilt. A large, old rug had seen far better days, and a small fireplace contained remnants of its last fire, probably decades earlier. Curtains, worn thin with age, fluttered at the wide-open window.

Gerda marched across the floor and pulled the window tightly shut.

The door slammed. Probably the draft from the window.

Gerda heard a long, low moan. It seemed to come from inside the room. She held her breath and waited.

The moan came again. Like a wounded animal.

She tiptoed to the small, open fireplace. It seemed louder here. Footsteps sounded along the corridor. She told herself one of the servants had come up. The door flew open.

Gerda let out a cry as a woman she didn't recognize stepped over the threshold.

"Who are you?" she demanded, glad her voice sounded strong.

"I have come to take you from this place. You no longer belong here."

The strange woman was dressed in a long scarlet gown. She wore a snake amulet, and her black hair was tightly braided. In an instant, Gerda realized she had seen her before.

"My God. You're in the painting. In the library."

The woman laughed and Gerda recoiled from the rotten teeth that had no place in such a beautiful woman.

"You are not destined to remain here. I have come to set you free."

"I don't understand, and I don't know what your game is, but I want you out of my house."

Again the woman laughed. "*Your* house? This has never been *your* house."

"Don't be ridiculous. I bought it. Cash. My family always pays cash."

The woman stopped laughing. Her eyes flashed. "This is not your house. You do not belong here. It returns to its rightful owner."

Gerda felt no fear, even though she thought she probably ought to. Her anger had risen to fever pitch. How dare this woman talk to her like this?

"*Who* are you?"

But the woman didn't reply.

A wave of nausea sent Gerda retching before she realized she was being transported, impossibly, through walls and space and down into the basement. Then she found herself in a room with a wall covered in ancient Egyptian hieroglyphics.

And over by that wall stood a man she vaguely recognized. Tall, bearded, dressed in an old-fashioned long jacket and a tall hat, like the one Abraham Lincoln used to wear. She had seen pictures of the president wearing such a hat when she was at school.

Gerda smelled smoke. From downstairs she heard screaming. The house. It must be on fire. "What have you done?"

The man said nothing. He stared at her, a look of utter contempt in his...

He saw her, but without eyes.

The lapsed Catholic crossed herself. "My God. Who are you? What have you done to me? To my home?"

The woman spoke. "It is better this way. Your spirit will be released to cross the desert and rest for all eternity."

"You intend to murder me?"

"No. Not murder. Not this time."

"What do you mean? Not this time?"

"Because you are already dead."

Chapter 16

Paula tried to take it in. "The buyer died seventy years earlier?"

"Yes. The new owner signed her name 'Elizabeth Charters' and the only Elizabeth Charters fitting the bill disappeared and, it is generally assumed, died in 1908. As I said, the signature on the document matches known samples of hers exactly."

"Don't tell me she disappeared in this house as well?"

"That is uncertain. She certainly wasn't seen after she had been in Egypt. She worked as assistant to Dr. Quintillus."

"*Him* again." Paula shook her head. "He's the reason this house is infested with evil."

"I cannot say," Stefan said.

Dee stayed silent.

"What else do you know?"

"Only that Count Markus didn't sell the house to Miss Charters. He sold it to Fräulein Gerda Zimic."

"Another name that keeps cropping up," Paula said. "Surely he must have noticed the signature? The discrepancy with the name?"

"It is believed he was so anxious to get out of the house that he didn't. He gave the document to his secretary, who promptly filed it without checking. It wasn't discovered until the family wanted to buy back the house and that was after the count's death—"

Anna's scream tore through the house.

Paula and Stefan found her, cowering at the entrance to the kitchen She pointed a shaking finger at the door leading to the basement.

Paula followed her terrified eyes. The carpenter stood rigid, transfixed. In his hand, he held a screwdriver, directed at his throat. All the tendons in his neck were stretched taut, as he struggled to fight off something that wanted him to harm himself. He yelled out in terror. Paula grabbed the hand that held the improvised weapon. With all her strength, she pulled, but it seemed nothing would stop the screwdriver from inching closer to the terrified man's jugular.

"Let go of him!" Paula redoubled her efforts. The man yelled out again and the screwdriver fell to the floor, narrowly missing Paula's foot. The carpenter fell backward, recovered himself, and rushed out of the kitchen, leaving his toolbox and its contents scattered across the floor.

"We're leaving," Paula said. "*Now*. Stefan, you have to get us out of this lease. I don't care how you do it, but we can't stay here another day."

Stefan nodded slowly. He seemed to be on autopilot. He spoke as if primed to do so. "I will drive you to a hotel. There is a good one near here."

"Right. Dee, pack up what you need for a couple of days, and I'll do the same. Anna, get yourself off home now. I'm so sorry you had to witness all that."

Anna's voice trembled. "And I am so sorry I can no longer work for you. Not here anyway. If you move somewhere else…"

"You would be the first one I'd call. Thank you for all you've done."

Anna managed a weak smile and left before Paula could change her mind. Stefan waited for them in the hallway. Paula shut the kitchen door firmly, wondering why she bothered. Whatever lay in wait here could easily break down locked and bolted doors, so one that was simply shut wouldn't stop it. She marched into the library and packed up her laptop before darting up the stairs to her bedroom. She ignored the unexpected chill and set to work throwing clothes and toiletries into a suitcase. Her nerve ends prickled. She felt unseen eyes watching her every move but, this time, instead of scaring her, it only spurred her to work faster.

She met Dee in the hall. She seemed to be taking it all in stride. Her calmness was almost unnerving.

"I'm a nervous wreck and you look like you would actually contemplate staying here."

Dee gave her a quick smile, which didn't last long enough to reach her eyes.

They followed Stefan to his car. He unlocked it and the sisters climbed in the back. Dee spoke. "At least we're unharmed and now we're leaving. End of story."

Paula looked at her hard. Her sister seemed different somehow. As if she had removed herself from the situation. This was a different Dee, and the subtle difference bothered Paula. Although for the life of her, she didn't know why.

———————

Paula and Dee checked into adjoining rooms in the smart, modern hotel. Paula unpacked and took a shower, keen to wash off every trace of Villa Dürnstein. Whatever resided there sullied everything it came into contact with and made her feel dirty and unhealthy.

Clean and dressed once more, she looked at her watch. It would be just after six in the morning in New York. Phil could well be up or might just be catching the last precious few minutes of sleep. Either way, she would have to call him before someone else told him she had asked Stefan to look into terminating the lease. She considered Skyping but abandoned the thought in favor of a straight phone call.

His tired voice answered on the fourth ring.

"Phil?"

"Paula? What the hell? I'm not even up yet. What's happened?"

"I know, and I'm sorry to wake you, but you will never believe the things that have been going on in the house."

"What?"

"Look, I won't go into all the details now, but I have had to ask Stefan to terminate the lease."

"You've done *what*?" *Now* he'd woken up.

"He was with us when it happened."

"When *what* happened?"

Paula tried to keep calm but couldn't stop her words tumbling out and, of course, it made no sense whatsoever to Phil. He could barely control the anger and shock in his voice. Maybe he wasn't even trying to.

"Phil, the place is haunted. And I mean badly. Really badly. All the crockery got smashed, the door to the basement was broken down, and a carpenter nearly killed himself with his own screwdriver."

"What the hell are you talking about, Paula? Have you been drinking? I'm going to call Stefan right now and tell him not to cancel the lease. Don't even think about it. Do you understand? Is Dee still there?"

"Yes. Quite honestly, I don't know what I'd do without her right now. At least she's here. She's seen it all for herself."

"I thought she was going back after a couple of days. What else haven't you been telling me? You said everything was fine when I spoke to you yesterday."

"I didn't want to worry you. I know how much you've got on your plate at the moment. I've hung on as long as I can, but things have escalated to the breaking point. Dee's staying on longer because she knows I need her. You're not here and—"

"I wondered when we would get onto that. I'm not having this conversation now. I've got to get to work."

"Phil. Don't call Stefan. We can't stay there. Dee and I are booked into a hotel now."

"*What?* Do you want me to be a laughingstock? The fucking Englishman with the crazy wife? You need help, Paula. Psychiatric help."

The urge to bite back was almost overwhelming. Why had he overreacted like that? Paula bit her lip. He was tired. The job in New York wasn't going well. He sounded exhausted. No, she mustn't lose her temper now. Quietly, she said, "Don't call me that. Anyone would be crazy to stay in that house after what's happened."

"I've had enough of this. I'm going. I'll talk to you again when you get your sanity back." He cut the call and left Paula clutching a dead phone, tears welling up.

Her tears had dried by the time she knocked on Dee's door, but she couldn't fool her own sister.

Dee took one look at Paula's reddened eyes and grabbed her hand. "Come on. We're going down to the bar and I'm buying you a drink." The old, caring Dee had returned.

Five minutes later, they sat in the comfortable lounge, surrounded by portraits of the Empress Elisabeth. Paula sipped from a large glass of Austrian Blaufränkisch while Dee nursed a brandy and soda.

"I gather you've spoken to Phil and it didn't exactly go well?" Dee said.

Paula raised her eyes heavenward. "To put it mildly. He went ballistic. He said he's telling Stefan not to release us from the lease."

"Shouldn't think he's too happy that I'm sticking around, either."

"Well…"

"You don't have to say any more. I get it."

"In his eyes, there's nothing wrong. Just two hysterical females winding each other up and making trouble for him. Plus, he's stressed at work."

"Oh dear, what a shame."

"Don't be sarcastic, Dee. He has a lot to contend with. His job makes him unpopular. Everyone eyes him with suspicion because they're sure he's looking for ways to either get them to work harder or else quit. He's found all sorts of stuff wrong in New York and somehow he's got to fix it. Then I come along and lay a whole load more trouble at his door at exactly the time he needs his home life to run smoothly."

"I can't believe you said that. I never took you for a Stepford wife."

"No, I didn't mean I have to play the good little housewife. God forbid he'd ever expect that. My German isn't good enough to get a job yet, so naturally, for the time being at least, the running of our home rests on my shoulders. It's my contribution. When I start work, things will change. He really doesn't need the prospect of another move so soon after we've arrived here, and he doesn't need to get a reputation for being difficult. They have rules about relocation and we're proposing to break practically every one of them."

"Except that in this instance, the house is uninhabitable."

"You and I know that. Stefan probably knows that now. But Phil doesn't."

"He could."

"What do you mean?"

"Supposing we go back to the house and Skype him. You could show him the damage. Then he'd have to believe you."

Paula took another sip of wine. Dee's suggestion made sense, but the thought of going back into that house so soon after this morning's events terrified her.

"Let me sleep on it, Dee. I really can't face it today."

"Fair enough. A bit of battery recharging would be a good idea, but promise me you'll consider it."

"I will. I promise."

After she had said goodnight to Dee, Paula booted up her laptop and checked her emails. Most of them were catalog offers and various other junk messages. One message stood out. Paula clicked on it.

It had been sent by a Professor Stephen Radford from Oxford University.

Dear Mrs. Bancroft. Thank you for your inquiry, which has been forwarded onto me. Dr. Emeryk Quintillus was employed here as you rightly believe. I can confirm, from information I have, that he was an eminent, if somewhat fanatical, archeologist. He went missing in 1910 and the university was informed by Dr. Quintillus's legal representatives that he had died. His last known location was Vienna, but he may have died in Egypt while engaged in one of his many digs. Of Professor Mayer, I know little as he was never employed by this university, although his reputation is highly regarded by all historians and archeologists, myself included. I am sorry not to have been able to add anything tangible to your existing knowledge, but it does appear that however deeply I dig, I fail to find much evidence of Dr. Quintillus's achievements. His character appears to have given considerable cause for alarm and disquiet among his academic colleagues, although he was highly regarded by many students. He seems to have angered many of his fellows and threatened at least one. I think if he were to apply for a position at this university in this day and age, the likelihood is he would be refused.

The professor signed himself off. Paula stared at the screen for a few seconds and closed it down.

―――――

Paula and Dee arrived at the Villa Dürnstein at midday the next day.

Paula checked her watch. It would be just after six a.m. in New York. She felt guilty Skyping Phil at this hour, especially after yesterday, but she couldn't see any viable alternative. He would be at work all day until God knows what time in the evening and she certainly didn't plan on hanging around this house after dark, waiting on the six-hour time difference.

"Are you ready?" Dee asked.

"Not really, but here goes anyway."

In the wrecked kitchen, they found everything exactly as it had been when they left yesterday. Paula took a deep breath and called her husband.

Seconds later, a bleary-eyed Phil, his hair disheveled, flashed up on the screen. "What is it now?"

"I have to show you this." She moved the phone around so her husband could see the damage. Dee stood silently in the doorway leading to the hall. From the phone, Phil's exclamation of horror filled the room.

"What the fuck's been going on there? An earthquake?"

"All sorts of crazy shit and no earthquake. You know how heavy that door is, how secure the locks were? This is what I tried to tell you about yesterday."

Dee grabbed the phone. "Phil, don't you care what's happening here? Your wife is being driven half-crazy by something we don't understand."

"Stay out of this, Dee. It's none of your business."

"My sister *is* my business. How dare you!"

Paula snatched the phone back. "Dee, it's okay. Phil, now you can see for yourself. We can't stay here."

Phil rubbed his eyes. Paula felt a wave of guilt and sympathy. He looked ten years older than his usual self. Things must be really hard for him over there.

"Paula," he said, his voice so low, almost menacing, it chilled his wife to the core. "We are not moving out. Stay in a hotel, if you must, until I get back—and get rid of that sister of yours."

Dee slammed her hand down hard on the table. "How *dare* you?"

Paula covered her sister's hand with her own. "Dee, please…" She shook her head, then turned back to Phil, whose jaw was set firmly in a way that Paula had always hated. "Phil, be reasonable. This is only the latest in a string of things that have been happening since you left. I didn't tell you because I know it's difficult for you over there and being so far away. But whatever is doing this is stepping things up, and I'm scared what it'll do next."

Phil sighed. "I called Stefan yesterday and he said you had become hysterical when he came over. He said nothing about ghosts or demons or whatever the hell it is you think is doing this stuff. He said as far as he could tell, the house had been broken into and he was getting it fixed."

Dee turned away.

Paula tried to remain calm. "I can't believe he said that. He saw what happened to the carpenter. The poor man was terrified."

"I don't know anything about a carpenter, but I do know we're not moving."

"But why not?"

"We would have to pay three years rent for a start."

"Surely not. There's always a get-out clause."

"Not this time. Why do you think it was so cheap?"

"I can't believe you signed up for something like that without even telling me what we were getting into."

Phil sighed. "I wanted you to have a lovely home. You supported me when I started out and this was my way of saying thank you. Look, I can't deal with this now. I'm due in a meeting across town in an hour. It'll take me that long just to get there. Stay in your hotel if you must. Go and see a doctor. Get yourself some pills to help you cope. Stefan will get the place fixed up again and when I get back, everything will be fine, okay?"

"No, Phil. It's not okay. I—"

"*Enough!*" He ended the call.

"I don't know how you live with that man," Dee said. "I'd have kicked him out years ago. Why on earth do you stay with him?"

"He's normally great and we get along fine. But when the two of you are in the same room—even electronically—it's like matter and anti-matter colliding."

"The way he spoke to you then. So patronizing. If a man treated me like that, he'd be history."

"He didn't mean it like that. He's just tired and he doesn't understand what's been happening."

"Make all the excuses for him you want, but there's no escaping the fact that he's not listening to you and, as a result, he's putting your life in danger."

"We don't know that. None of us has been injured."

"Yet. Supposing it had been a screwdriver in *your* hand, pointing at *your* throat. The carpenter wrenched himself free but supposing you weren't able to and I wasn't there to help you."

Paula didn't want to imagine it. She wanted only to get her things and leave. "I'll pop upstairs and get a few more clothes. Do you need anything?"

"I've got everything. At the hotel. You didn't think I intended to come back here after yesterday, did you? It's only because this was the only way, and even this didn't work. That man is so pigheaded."

Paula didn't want another argument at that moment. "I'll be a few minutes."

Upstairs, she grabbed a suitcase out of the closet and began piling in more clothes. She struggled to close the bulging case and finally succeeded as a scream from downstairs tore through the house.

"*Dee.*" She hurried out of the room and down the stairs. She found Dee sprawled out in a dead faint between the kitchen and hallway.

"Dee, wake up." Paula took her hand between both of hers and began rubbing it. Her sister stirred, groaned and her eyes fluttered open. At first she seemed disoriented, unable to articulate.

"Where...?"

"It's all right, Dee. You fainted. What happened?"

"Happened?" She looked confused. Her words seemed to come hard. "I don't know. I..." Her eyes closed briefly and she frowned, as if struggling to remember.

"Did you see something?" Paula said.

Dee's eyes opened again. "See something?"

"Did something…appear?"

Dee struggled to sit up. "I don't know…what…you're talking about."

Paula's heartbeat quickened. She could almost have been talking to a stranger. Dee barely appeared to recognize her and her words came hard—as if she was struggling with what to say.

"It doesn't matter. Try and stand. I'll get you a glass of water." Paula helped her up and, leaning heavily on her sister, Dee made it to a chair in the hallway. She sank down untidily.

Paula poured a tumbler of water and handed it to her. "I think this is the only glass that escaped destruction," she said, trying to lighten the mood.

Dee sipped her drink. She stared at the floor and said nothing. Color gradually returned to her blanched face, but still she did not speak. Paula took the empty glass from her, fear mounting.

"Dee, are you okay?" Her sister didn't react. "Dee?" Paula took her hand. Dee raised her eyes. She seemed not to see her sister. "You're worrying me now."

Dee shook off her hand and got up unsteadily. On shaky legs, she made her way along the hall. She stopped by a mirror and stared at herself for a moment, stroking her hair as if rediscovering herself.

"We'd better get you to the hospital and have them check you out," Paula said. "You might have a concussion."

Dee looked at her. "I am quite well," she said, but her voice sounded strange.

"I'm not happy, Dee. You're not yourself."

"I can assure you I am."

"You're acting weird."

Dee pulled herself up, seeming to make a concerted effort to get herself back together. This time, when she spoke, the old Dee returned.

"Must have had a sudden drop in blood pressure or something. I feel much better now. Let's get out of this place."

Paula didn't need telling twice.

Back at the hotel, after a hearty dinner of Tafelspitz topped off with a bottle of Burgenland's finest, Paula felt exhausted. Her eyes kept closing.

Dee stood up from the table, swayed and put a hand to her head. Paula jumped to her feet. "Are you okay? It's not the same as earlier, is it?"

Dee looked at her blankly. "Earlier?"

"Yes, you remember. At the house a few hours ago. You fainted."

"Oh. No. I'll be all right in a minute. Just stood up too quickly, that's all."

"As long as that's all there is to it."

Dee managed a smile. "I'll be fine. I need some sleep."

Paula settled Dee in her room and returned to her own. She switched on the TV and tried to follow the news in German as best she could.

She stared at her phone, willing Phil to call her, but he would still be at work.

At midnight, she got ready for bed and had slipped under the duvet when her phone announced a Skype call.

Phil had undone his collar and removed his tie. He had dark shadows under his eyes as if he hadn't slept for days.

"Paula. Have you sent that sister of yours packing yet?"

"No, I haven't, and I don't intend to until you get back."

Why did they have to argue like this when they were so far apart?

Phil let out a deep, somewhat exaggerated, sigh. "I'm calling to tell you that I've managed to rectify the damage you've done and Stefan has arranged for the kitchen to be repaired, appliances and utensils replaced, and the door to be fixed."

"Let's hope that his men don't have the same experience as that unfortunate carpenter."

"Paula, please. Will you stop with this mumbo jumbo?"

"I'd be delighted if that's all it was."

"There's clearly no talking to you when you're in this mood. I thought you should know what's going on at the house. That's all." Once again, he ended the call.

———

"Dee, are you sure you're all right?" Paula set down a cup of coffee in front of her. She ignored it and continued to stare straight in front of her in the hotel breakfast room. "Dee?"

Her sister blinked and seemed to shake herself from whatever trance she had slipped into.

"Yes?"

"You were miles away then. I asked if you were all right. You've been a bit…distant since you fainted back at the house. I still think we should get to the hospital and have you checked over."

"Hospital? I don't need a hospital. I am perfectly well. When are we going back?"

"Back?"

"To the house."

"Dee, we're not going back."

She looked as if Paula had slapped her face.

"But you live there. We shouldn't be staying in this hotel."

"After what happened to you? After everything that's happened there? Are you serious?"

Dee stared at her. Paula felt Dee had left and a total stranger had taken her place.

"I'm sorry. Yes. You're right, of course. We can't go back there."

The almost robotic tone took Paula off-guard. She seemed to be reciting the words or reading them off some invisible teleprompter. They were sitting by a large picture window. Out of the corner of her eye, Paula glimpsed a large black cat strolling past. She turned her head to get a better look, but it had gone.

Dee stood up. "Let's go."

"Go? Go where?"

"Anywhere. Let's get some fresh air. Clear my head."

"Of course." Paula pushed her chair back. Dee had already left the table.

————

They crossed the street to the U-bahn and went down the stairs to the city center—bound platform. A train arrived almost immediately and, without a word being exchanged, they boarded and sat next to each other.

"Where do you want to go today?" Paula asked.

Dee shrugged her shoulders. "Your call."

"Okay," Paula thought for a moment. "How about a stroll along Kärntnerstrasse? There are some great shops and we can take it easy. Plenty of places to stop for coffee and something to eat."

Dee nodded. "Sounds good."

Any less enthusiasm would have been hard to imagine. Paula sighed. Dee could be moody. As a child, she used to scream her head off if she was crossed. Paula used to stick her fingers in her ears to drown out the piercing screech. At sixteen, Dee would sulk but, as she grew older, the moodiness lessened and a fiery temper developed. Fortunately, it rarely came out. She did, of course, make an exception for Phil. Everything he said or did seemed to press her fury button. Today's indifference to everything was uncharacteristic.

Vienna's expensive shopping street was, as usual, packed with tourists. Japanese, Italian, German, French, American, Australian, British… Paula had only been off the train five minutes and she had heard all those languages and accents, plus some she didn't recognize. Smells of pizza, and aromas of an array of coffee and freshly cooked street food mingled with the expensive perfumes tourists had acquired at the duty-free.

Paula broke the silence between them. "Would you like to go into the cathedral? I haven't been yet and, from the pictures I've seen, it's well worth a visit."

"Fine with me."

"Dee, for heaven's sake, what's wrong with you?"

The two sisters faced each other.

"If you must know," Dee said, her eyes flashing anger, "I think we should go back to the house and face up to whatever is in there."

"What? Why?"

"Because sooner or later it's going to come for you. And me probably. You remember that guy in the Café Central, and the woman in the Palace? I've never been a fan of coincidences, and for two people to say they saw a ghost with us…two total strangers—"

"You may not be a fan of them, but coincidences do happen. And anyway, one reported seeing a ghostly woman and the other a ghost of a man. Not the same thing at all."

"I think we'd better go and get a coffee. This might take a while." Dee led Paula to Café Demel in a side street. Stepping through its original eighteenth-century doorway, Paula felt transported into an age of timeless elegance. It calmed her for a moment at least, and she needed that calm more than she dared admit.

They ordered mélanges and when they arrived, Dee took a sip of hers. "Delicious."

"Okay, Dee, you've got me here, tell me what's on your mind."

Dee inhaled. "Here goes. When we were in the Café Central and that man described seeing a male ghost, his description sounded an awful lot like what I thought I saw."

"Quintillus, presumably."

"It was supposedly standing right behind you. Then in the palace, that girl said she saw a ghostly woman behind me. In both cases we were nowhere near your house. These ghosts had come with us. Whatever you say, I don't think you can simply walk away from it. I don't think I can, either."

Dee had only said what Paula herself now feared, but she wished she could have spared her sister the worry. She made one last feeble effort. "That's always assuming those people weren't off their heads."

It didn't work. "Oh, come on, Paula. How many times previously have you been told there was a ghost standing behind you?"

"None."

"Precisely. But now you get two in two days. Doesn't that strike you as even a little odd?"

"Of course it does, but I don't understand why you think we need to go back to the house."

Dee put her hand to her head. She visibly paled.

Paula leaned forward. "Admit it, you're not well, are you?"

Dee dropped her hand to her side. "I shall be fine once this is dealt with."

"And how do you propose to do that? We're way out of our depth here."

"Somebody's got to know what to do. What about your cleaner? Anna? She knows people at the university, doesn't she?"

"Former cleaner now, I'm afraid. And she only knows people who know the legends. I doubt she knows any professionals, psychics or whatever it is we need. We're in a foreign country, Dee. Neither of us speaks more than a few words of German, and while so many people speak English here, we're not talking about your usual day-to-day stuff. I wouldn't have a clue where to start."

"Phil speaks German, doesn't he?"

"You know he does. His parents brought him up bilingual. That's how he got the posting here. But don't start thinking he'll do anything to help. You've seen him. He's a complete skeptic about this, even though some strange stuff had started happening before he left for New York. Now he's barely speaking to me."

"Stefan then. I know he's not ideal, but he saw what happened at the house."

"And, according to Phil, he's now denying there was anything supernatural going on. I tried to call him to demand an explanation but he was out for the rest of the day."

"You're sure Phil wasn't saying that simply to put you off?"

Paula wasn't sure. She hoped with all her heart he had told her the truth, but he had been so adamant they weren't moving, could he have made it up?

"I'll call Stefan in the morning, get him to explain himself and see if he knows anyone who can speak English and who knows how to cleanse a house."

"It'll need more than that," Dee said. "I think we need an exorcist."

Paula couldn't recall when she had last been rendered speechless, but her sister accomplished that now. Jumbled thoughts, words, questions all tumbled into her brain, but she could voice none of them. Dee put a hand on her arm.

"I didn't want to say this," she said, "but I think things have gone too far for me to keep quiet about it any longer."

Finally, Paula found her voice. "What do you mean? Keep quiet about what?"

"What's been happening to you. The nightmares, the kitchen…everything really."

"Go on."

"Those weren't nightmares, Paula. They were real. You experienced every single one of them. I know because I saw you."

"I…don't understand, and what has this got to do with getting an exorcist? Surely they deal with people who believe they're possessed by an evil spirit. None of us is possessed here."

"I'm afraid that's not true, is it?"

"Dee, whatever you're trying to say, come out with it. I don't get where you're coming from."

"Okay. I'll try. Give me a moment."

Dee laid her hands flat on the table. "You're going to have a hard time with this, but I'm going to say it anyway. Paula, there's something inside you. As soon as you moved into that house, an entity entered your body and took possession of it. I don't believe you're aware of it yourself, but it's still there."

Twice in one day, Paula lost her capacity for speech. Dee stared at her, unsettling Paula even more. "Have you lost your mind?" she said eventually.

Dee shook her head. "If only it were that easy. All the evidence points to it. The manifestations. The destruction. Everything. It's coming from inside you."

"Where the hell did you get that idea from?" Paula realized she had raised her voice. People at a nearby table were beginning to take an interest in their conversation. She lowered her voice again. "This is the craziest idea you've ever come up with. What would make you say such a thing?"

Dee leaned in. "Because it's happened before."

"*What*?"

The people at the next table openly stared. *Let them.*

"You won't remember because you're not supposed to. When we were kids, you had an imaginary friend. Chloe. You used to go everywhere with her."

Paula had an impression of having walked out of her life and into someone else's. Nothing Dee said rang any bells or stirred any memories.

"I don't remember any imaginary friend."

"As I said. You're not supposed to. Chloe was your confidante. She came between you and me, and I grew so jealous of her. That didn't matter to you, though, because she was all you cared about at that time. Mum and Dad weren't concerned. They said imaginary friends were normal as a child. But it meant I had no one to play with anymore and I became increasingly angry about it. *She* didn't like that, and that's when things began to change. I began to see a ghostly shadow, holding your hand. She gradually became more solid over the next few weeks. A tall girl with dark hair. Quite attractive and a number of years older than you, but she could change. Then her face would become darker and I grew to fear that change because that's when she would hurt me."

Paula grew increasingly incredulous the more she heard. None of it sounded familiar, but her sister plowed on. Now she had started, she didn't want to stop. That, at least, was obvious.

"At first she pinched me, or pulled my hair. Then she smashed my favorite doll to pieces. Mum became concerned and when she saw you cutting up my dolls' clothes, she knew this had become much more serious than any imaginary friend. You insisted Chloe had done it and that's when she lost her temper. I never saw Mum so angry, either before or since. She marched you off to a child psychiatrist and he diagnosed multiple personality disorder or some such thing. I overheard Mum and Dad talking about it. You were put on tranquilizers and for a time all went quiet. We even started getting our relationship back. You played with me sometimes, but I was always wary of Chloe returning. Of course, I didn't tell Mum that your imaginary friend actually existed. I suppose that was cowardly of me, but I didn't want them thinking I had gone mad as well."

Paula flinched at the use of that word. "So, what happened? Why can't I remember any of this?"

"You know Mum always clung to her Catholic roots? Dad went along with her. They found an exorcist. A priest. He performed a ritual cleansing of the house and tackled the evil spirit that had possessed you. You struggled a great deal and kept screaming out in some language none of the adults could understand but, somehow, up in my bedroom where I'd been instructed to stay, I could both hear and understand the spirit's words. They came to me in my head. Whatever possessed you had ancient scores to settle. It told me it would leave you for now but would come back when the time was right. That's all I know."

"Dee, are you sure you're not making all this up? It's the most incredible, preposterous story I've ever heard, and I certainly would never have expected to hear such words coming from you."

"What possible reason would I have for lying?"

"I have no idea, but if I find out you are... Look, you've always been the practical, down-to-earth one of the pair of us. Ghosts, demons, evil spirits had no place in our vocabulary until you came here."

"And do you know why that is? Because after your session with the exorcist, I was warned never to mention the supernatural around you. The priest had put a suggestion to you under hypnosis, wiping out all your memories of Chloe and everything she had supposedly done. He feared that any exposure to talk about the paranormal, especially while you were so young and impressionable, might trigger everything again, so if you ever mentioned anything vaguely paranormal, I always changed the subject."

"Or poured ridicule all over it."

Dee nodded. "Frequently both."

The whole thing sounded crazy. How could all this have happened in her childhood and she not remember any of it? Paula searched her mind for answers, but none came—apart from one.

"So, what you're saying," she began, "is that for some reason you don't understand, the entity that was apparently sleeping inside me has now woken up."

"That's probably the best way to put it."

It didn't ring true. "How do you know it isn't you who is possessed?"

"Because of what I just told you. It's returned because the time is right. I don't know what that means, but..."

"Maybe it's returned, but in you. After all, that girl did say the female ghost was standing behind you."

Dee nodded. "True. But I don't have the history. You do. Anyway, never mind that. Give Stefan a call and see if he can help us."

Paula stared at her sister for a moment before reaching into her purse for her phone.

Stefan sounded mildly surprised to receive a call from her.

"Your husband told me you do not wish to cancel the lease," he said.

"He doesn't. I do. Stefan, why did you tell my husband that nothing supernatural was going on in our house? After everything you saw?"

A pause. "I did not say that to him."

"He told me you said it was a burglary."

"I'm sorry, Mrs. Bancroft. But that isn't true."

Paula saw no further point in arguing. He was adamant, and right now she had more pressing problems.

With a great effort, she said, "We need an exorcist. Urgently."

"*Exorzist?* I am sorry, I do not know any…exorcists…but I can ask people."

"Please, as quickly as you can."

Paula put the phone down and pushed her coffee to one side. Dee drained her cup.

"He said he would help," Paula said. "But he denies saying anything to Phil about a burglary. All of a sudden, I need something stronger. Much stronger." She summoned a waiter and ordered them both a brandy.

"I have found someone to help you," Stefan said.

She held her phone closer to her ear.

"Her name is Lena Stein. She speaks excellent English and she is, I don't know in English, a *spiritistische medium*."

"A medium? That sounds right. When can we meet her?"

"She says it is important to meet her at the house. The Villa Dürnstein. She says it must be where things happen."

"I wish to God I didn't have to go back to that place."

"She is most adamant. It must be the house. The repairs are complete now and I restocked the kitchen with everything you should need, apart from fresh food of course."

"And the door to the basement?"

"It has been replaced. I spoke to the family, told them what had happened and they were most concerned. A new door is now fixed. It is steel, on their instructions."

Paula breathed an inward sigh of relief. Surely nothing would get through a steel door. So why couldn't she fully believe it? And right now, that wasn't the only thing troubling her. What the hell was going on with Dee? And what about all this talk of some ghostly friend from her past? Paula massaged her throbbing head.

———

Dee and Paula arrived at the house and let themselves in through the front door. The smell of spring flowers greeted them and the reason for it soon presented itself. A massive bowl of freesias and an assortment of less familiar but wonderfully scented flowers accompanied them.

"There's a card," Dee said, and handed it to her sister.

Paula slipped it out of the envelope. "'To welcome you back to your home. I trust all will be in order and thank you for your understanding. Stefan Bloch.'"

"That's very nice of him," Dee said.

"Yes," said Paula, tapping her teeth with the card. "And unexpected, too."

"Maybe his conscience is pricking him."

"Maybe." Paula shivered. The doorbell rang.

"That'll be her," Dee said.

"I'll get it." Paula was already at the door. She opened it and a woman of roughly her own age smiled at her on the doorstep.

"Frau Bancroft? I am Lena. Stefan told you I am coming, yes?"

"Yes, please come in, Frau Stein."

"Please, call me Lena."

"I'm Paula, and this is my sister, Dee."

Dee stepped forward and stuck her hand out. Lena politely declined the contact. "I must not shake hands or touch anyone until after my work is complete."

Paula and Dee exchanged glances out of her eyeline.

Lena had already started toward the library. "This I think is the right room."

Paula caught up with her at the door. "Possibly, but the really frightening stuff kicked off in the kitchen and seemed to come from the basement."

Lena turned her brilliant smile on her. "Later, perhaps. Now I think we start in here. I feel something quite powerful is in this room."

As soon as Lena stepped into the library and caught sight of the ceiling, she hugged herself. Then she caught sight of the portrait on the wall. She approached it—and recoiled.

"What's the matter? Is it the painting?"

Lena nodded. "It is powerful."

"Gustav Klimt painted it," Dee said. "Beautiful, isn't it?"

"It is a vile thing. A cursed thing." Lena crossed herself and backed away. She glanced swiftly up at the ceiling and hurriedly crossed herself again. She whispered under her breath and Paula guessed she was praying.

Lena clutched a plain gold crucifix she wore around her neck.

"Lena, can you help us?" Paula asked, aware of the pleading tone in her voice.

Lena turned frightened eyes toward them. "I… I don't know. I try. You are right. Not in here. In the kitchen."

She ran out of the room, still clutching the crucifix. She didn't need pointing in the right direction, either. She made straight for the kitchen.

"What was that all about?" Paula asked Dee, who shrugged her shoulders.

In the kitchen, Lena poured herself a glass of water. Paula looked around. Stefan had done a good job. The room sparkled once again, and the new steel door didn't look out of place among the gleaming chrome. It certainly appeared substantial enough. There were no padlocks this time, but a heavy-duty combination lock.

"I am sorry," Lena said. "The force in that room is too powerful. I feel it pulling me. If I allow it, I think it might kill me. It wants to use me. I don't know why. I will help you all I can but I must not go into that room and you must not also. My guide has warned me."

"What sort of force?" Paula asked. "Is it the painting on the ceiling, or the one on the wall?"

"Both I think, but the smaller one. The one on the wall. That is the most powerful of all. It should not be there. It wants to be there, but it must be destroyed. If you can destroy it."

"But it's an original Klimt," Dee said.

Lena flashed her an angry glance. "The painter hated that picture. It is not natural."

"How do you know?" Paula asked.

"His hate is in every brushstroke. Hate. And fear."

If she hadn't been so serious, Paula might have found it absurd. Amusing, even. But Lena *was* serious. "I found it in the basement," she said.

"I know," Lena said. "That is where *he* is."

A cloak of ice descended around Paula. Dee said nothing.

"Who is?" Paula asked, already guessing the answer.

Lena blinked steadily. "Emeryk Quintillus. He is alive."

Chapter 17

"*A*live?" Surely Paula had misunderstood. "But that's impossible."

Lena shook her head. "For most people, yes. For him, no. Achillas, my spirit guide, tells me. He is not like other men. He has walked in the darkness and shadows for many years. One life ends and another begins. He is alive but not as you or I. Someone helps him. Always there is someone who helps him. For a price."

"You've lost me again," Paula said. Dee still said nothing. Probably as baffled as she was.

"He has help from one who is to walk the earth. Without end. She searches for revenge. She thinks she gets it, and it slips through her fingers."

"Who is she?"

"The sister of Cleopatra. Arsinoe."

"And your spirit guide...Achillas? He's told you all this?" Paula asked.

Lena nodded, looked up and spread her arms wide. "It is in this house. In the walls. Achillas is warning me to go now. I am not protected. No one is protected in this house. Tomorrow I will come back and I will bring what I can to help me. Until I can—if I can—remove this evil, you must not stay here. It is all I can do to protect you for now. I have great fear that it will not be enough. His evil is so strong and her power is great. She can leave this house. Perhaps he can, too. They can travel. I don't know. I can only see what is in this house, and what I see is pure evil."

"What is this price you said Arsinoe demands? Can Achillas tell you that?"

Lena closed her eyes. She seemed to be listening. A slight nod, and she opened her eyes again. "She seeks revenge against the sister who killed her. Cleopatra's spirit lies, with her lover, Mark Antony, near her. Close enough so she can feel his presence. It brings her peace. Arsinoe hates that. She wants her sister to suffer as she suffers. To walk endlessly through eternity, alone. Arsinoe... I don't know the word...*trösten*."

"Trust?"

Lena shook her head. "No, no. She feels bad and wants..." Lena mimicked hugging, stroking her face and patting.

"Console. She wants to console herself."

"I think...maybe...yes. Console herself. Arsinoe takes a human... Goes into someone."

Dee spoke for the first time. "Possesses? She possesses another person. Another woman's body." She looked meaningfully at Paula.

Paula flinched. The evil spirit of a vengeful Arsinoe in her? Wouldn't she be aware of it?

Lena nodded and fixed Dee with a stare. "*Genau*. Exactly." A sudden frown, a moment's confusion perhaps, creased her forehead. "I must go now. Please also leave with me."

Paula did not need urging. She locked the door behind them. On the doorstep, Lena took her hand. Ignoring Dee, she said, "Be very careful. I come back tomorrow at the same time."

Paula nodded and the woman scurried away.

"What do you make of that?" Paula asked Dee.

"Seemed a bit farfetched, but then everything about this house stretches credibility to its outer limits."

"You're right there. Come on, let's get back to the hotel. A glass of wine beckons."

Yet again, Phil's phone went to voicemail. Paula checked her watch. One a.m. Seven p.m. in New York. Surely he had arrived home by now. This was the third day in a row she hadn't spoken to him. It hurt all the more because the last time she had, they had parted so acrimoniously. She rang again. Voicemail.

She had given up leaving messages after her fifth. If he didn't know she was worried by now, he never would. She threw the cell onto the bed. Tears filled her eyes. If only they hadn't come to Vienna. Everything had been fine before.

Paula's dreams were tortured. Each one brought her back to the Villa Dürnstein. In one she floated there on a night such as the one she now slept through. Clear, chilly with a light breeze that ruffled her hair and nightdress. She tripped on the front step and lost her slipper. She retrieved it and found she had stepped in some mud. It clung to the toweling fabric and she rubbed it off her hands.

The front door stood open. The man she felt sure was Quintillus waited for her in the hallway. Fear coiled through every nerve and sinew in her body. She had to get away from him. She must run. With a crash, the door slammed behind her. The man came closer. But not alone.

A giant figure, part man, part animal towered above her. His head appeared almost to be a dog, but the ears were tall and stood erect on top of its head. He carried a staff in one hand and an ankh in the other. She recognized him immediately. The god Set. He raised his staff and the house shook to its foundations. A screaming wind tore through the building, knocking Paula off her feet and propelling her into the kitchen. The basement door had vanished and the wind flung her through the entrance. Here, complete stillness. In front of her, the steps led down into darkness. Around her, the sickly stench of lilies and death made her retch.

She couldn't escape. Set barred the entrance. She would have to go down.

Paula took hold of the handrail and felt her way from one step to the next into the unrelieved blackness. At the foot of the stairs, she listened. Nothing. A pinprick of light struck the floor ahead of her, illuminating it enough to enable her to see her way forward. She made her way toward it, straining to hear any sound, but heard none. She crept along, the light maintaining an even distance ahead of her. The wall that had marked the end of the corridor had vanished and, in its place, an old doorway led to a room. The scene rippled in front of her.

She didn't anticipate the sudden light that scythed through the blackness. She shielded her eyes. Candles flickered, casting eerie shadows on the wall, illuminating the hieroglyphics. A large cat stood proudly, its unblinking stare appearing to weigh Paula up. It remained so still she wasn't sure it was real until it blinked its astonishing eyes.

Quintillus had made it there ahead of her. He directed whatever sight he was capable of at her. A woman joined him. She stood, bathed in shadow so that Paula could not distinguish her features.

Paula's bare feet felt numb with cold as she stood on the dirty stone floor. The sickening stench invaded every pore of her body and her stomach heaved.

"What am I doing here?" she asked.

No one answered.

"I have a right to know why you are doing this to me. To my sister."

The woman slowly moved out of the shadows and toward Paula. When she saw her, Paula let out a gasp.

"*Dee.*"

Paula awoke, bathed in sweat. Like the others, this nightmare felt so real. She grabbed a tissue from the box by the bedside and mopped her brow. When she had finished, she caught sight of her slippers on the floor and let out a gasp.

They were caked in mud. And her hand was streaked with it.

―――――

Dee looked up from her coffee and frowned. "You look pale. Didn't you sleep well?"

"Nightmare. But it was so strange. I dreamed I walked through mud, and this morning my slippers and my hand were caked with it."

"What? How did that happen?"

Paula shook her head. "You were there. In my nightmare."

"I don't know whether I should be flattered or insulted." Dee let out a light laugh. "I hope I wasn't the villain of the piece."

Paula didn't reply. Her head throbbed and she left Dee to get some fresh orange juice and strong coffee from the buffet. The thought of eating anything turned her stomach. None of her thoughts made sense today. Maybe they would after they met up with Lena at the house, but the thought of going back there filled her with dread. She rejoined Dee, who was finishing off a croissant.

"Is that all you're having? You'll be starved later."

"I'll be fine. Maybe when I've drunk this coffee I'll feel like something more substantial."

But she didn't.

Lena had already arrived and stood on the doorstep. This time she carried a small suitcase. She greeted Paula with a half-smile that failed to include Dee. "I hope I have everything I need. I spend all night praying we shall succeed today."

Paula let them in. The house smelled different than yesterday. She wrinkled her nose. "It's like rotting vegetables."

"The flowers," Dee exclaimed. "They've all died. How is that possible since yesterday?"

Lena addressed her reply to Paula. "It is the evil in this house," she said, hugging herself. "It wants nothing to live. Only itself."

Paula wanted nothing more than to run as far away as she could from that place. "I'll clear the mess up later," she said, eyeing the withered leaves, the fallen blooms and scattered brown petals. "Let's get this over with, shall we?"

Lena nodded. "We go to the kitchen."

She motioned Paula and Dee to sit with her around the small kitchen table. From her suitcase, she produced a small bottle. "Holy water," she said. Then she reached in and took out a Bible, small black book, sagebrush, matches and a pentacle on a gold chain. "Now we hold hands, please."

"Isn't this a bit Hollywood?" Dee asked.

Lena glared at her.

"It's only that yesterday you said you mustn't touch anyone until your work was done and today you're holding our hands."

"I know more today than yesterday." Her tone had turned snappy. She closed her eyes.

Dee raised her eyebrows at Paula, who motioned her to keep quiet.

Paula winced as Lena's grip tightened. She saw Dee do the same. Once again, her skin began to prickle.

Lena mouthed something inaudible.

A hollow groan echoed through the house. Timbers creaked.

Lena dropped their hands and opened her eyes. Paula massaged some life back into her cramped fingers.

"Do not speak," Lena said to Dee, who looked as if she might. "It is near to us."

A loud ripping sound came from beyond the hall.

A crash.

The foul smell of excrement swept into the kitchen. Paula and Lena retched, but Dee seemed oblivious.

To Paula's horror, a shape formed in the doorway. The more it manifested itself, the darker the kitchen became.

"Dr. Quintillus," Lena said.

Paula gasped as the figure moved. He seemed to be walking, but his boots made no sound on the tiled floor. Paula recognized him instantly. Emeryk Quintillus, his expressionless face gray and withered, stood in front of them. So the nightmares had been real. She flinched from his sightless gaze.

Lena stood, picked up her Bible, opened it and began to read in rapid German.

Quintillus laughed. His mouth, full of rotten teeth, opened as he roared with joyless, echoing laughter that chilled Paula.

The Bible flew out of Lena's hands and thumped against the wall.

Lena picked up the sagebrush and reached for the matches. They skittered across the table and landed on the floor. The box opened and scattered the contents far and wide.

Lena hadn't finished yet. She picked up the holy water but she had to fight for control of it. The black holes in Quintillus's face blazed with red fire. The water began to bubble. With a cry of pain, Lena dropped it. It smashed on the table and boiling water spread in a pool.

Dee moaned and pointed to the door into the hallway.

A tall young woman in a flowing red gown held a gold dagger in her hand. *Arsinoe.* Horrified, Paula cried out as she raised her arm and pointed the weapon at Dee.

Dee cried out. "No, I won't."

The dagger flew end over end into Dee's hand, so that her sister now brandished it.

Dee stared helplessly at her sister. "I'm so sorry, Paula." Her hand tightened around the hilt of the dagger. "I can't control this. I couldn't control any of it once *they* took over. All that stuff I told you…"

In an instant, everything fell into place. The inconsistent way her sister had been behaving. The stories from their childhood… "All that stuff about an imaginary friend. It didn't happen, did it?"

Dee shook her head, tears coursing down her face. "They put the words there. I almost believed it myself. And there's more…so much more. I shouldn't have…" The humanity faded from her eyes, replaced by a flashing white light as Arsinoe stepped forward to claim her prize.

The girl vanished and an unfamiliar light shone through Dee's eyes.

Quintillus stepped aside.

Paula knew what she had to do. She threw herself at Arsinoe, now fully in her sister's body, taking her by surprise. She knocked the dagger out of her hand and it clattered away across the floor.

"You will not have her," Paula cried as she grappled with her.

Lena opened her black book and screamed incantations in German.

Paula yelled at her, "Make it go away."

Arsinoe flung Paula away from her and she collapsed against the wall, pain screaming up her back. She struggled to right herself as Arsinoe joined Quintillus.

He raised his hand and clenched his fist.

Lena dropped the book. She collapsed on the floor. Arsinoe and Quintillus bent over her, appearing to inhale her last breath. They had turned away from Paula.

Paula saw her chance and took it. With strength she summoned from somewhere, she grabbed the dagger and staggered out of the kitchen toward the library. She shut the door and locked it. With no idea of what to do next, she glanced upward at the painting. The girl in the scarlet gown had gone.

A noise behind her made her turn. Quintillus and Arsinoe stood side by side. Paula froze at the woman's words as she spoke to her companion.

"Now I live, you shall have your reward as I promised."

Quintillus moved closer to Paula. His voice dry and brittle, he said, "You are sure?"

"I am sure."

Arsinoe waved her arm and a large black cat appeared. It sat beside her, its face taking on the semblance of a lion, while its fur changed from jet black to gleaming golden. It stood on two legs. Its paws morphed and, from the neck down, robes of green, scarlet, and gold replaced the fur. The goddess Sekhmet stood silently. Waiting. As Paula continued to be rooted to the spot, a shadow appeared on the wall. It took mere seconds for the god Set to emerge. He, too, stood silently.

"Now it begins," Arsinoe said.

A sound of crackling, snapping and a loud sigh came from the portrait on the wall.

Paula could do nothing. She could neither move nor think clearly. Her thoughts muddied themselves. Visions of an Egypt where men and women walked dusty streets looking as if they had stepped out of a museum. And she had become one of them. No, not one of them.

She ruled them. She wanted to stay there. In the great temple that soared above her. She wanted to remain where her lover lay nearby—somewhere just out of reach.

But something dragged her from there. Against her will. It must not happen. They could not take her. Not again.

Sekhmet's hypnotic eyes drew her ever further. She fought and it pulled harder.

She cried out. "I am the queen. I shall always be the queen." Had she really spoken those words? No, not her. Someone else. And now she floated, drifted. A beautiful goddess in a golden chariot awaited her. But Paula felt another presence. A far more sinister entity. It lurked just out of sight, biding its time.

From somewhere far away, Arsinoe laughed. "You can do nothing. I am your queen now, and you will obey me."

Paula heard another voice. It came from her body.

"Isis protect me. Set protect me."

"The gods have deserted you, treacherous sister," Arsinoe said. "I have the power of Set and Sekhmet. You shall remain trapped here, inside this body, far from the man you love, bound to a man obsessed with you."

Paula willed herself back into her body, but a new force barred her way. On the edge of her vision, out of reach, the beautiful goddess beckoned to her. She felt a strong sense of peace emanating from the deity she recognized as Isis. It wrapped itself around her. She wanted only to give herself up to it, to allow herself to be swept away into the afterlife.

But darkness swept in from the outer edge of time. It came as a shadow so black she couldn't penetrate it. However hard she tried, Paula could no longer see the goddess.

A hideous beast threw off its cloak of shadow. It reared up in front of her—charcoal colored, scaly, its long fangs protruding from a lipless mouth. The atmosphere around her froze.

Despair filled her spirit and washed away hope.

Paula's world went black.

Chapter 18

When Cleopatra opened her eyes, she lay on a floor in an unfamiliar room. A stranger bent over her. No, not a stranger. She had seen this one before. He had imprisoned her before. She looked about her at the strange furniture. Not of her time, or her place. And this man…

Mists cleared in her mind and she remembered. A woman, driven from her body. *This* body. Her own spirit forced into it, though she fought against it.

She cried out in her new voice. *"No."*

He took her hand and her touch seemed to revive his withered skin. In an instant, empty veins pulsed once more with circulating blood. Healthy, supple skin covered his face and hands.

He kissed her hand, and she withdrew it in disgust.

"My queen. You are returned to me."

"Never."

She staggered forward, her new body only reluctantly obeying her commands. A dagger lay a few feet away from her. The man called Quintillus didn't appear to have noticed it. He made to steady her, but she shrugged his hand off.

In an instant, she crouched and managed to save herself from toppling over. She snatched up the dagger. Quintillus wrestled her for it.

She lashed out at him, the dagger scything through the air. "You cannot imprison me here." She caught the side of his face. A thin stream of blood ran down his cheek. He lunged for her arms but she sidestepped him.

"You took me once before. You shall not do so again. I curse you, Emeryk Quintillus. You are damned for all time." Cleopatra plunged the dagger deep into her chest. She staggered. Collapsed. Blood pooled around her, and her spirit was released.

Quintillus sank to his knees and let out a howl of anguish.

In the basement, Arsinoe smiled. "No, my sister, you do not escape so easily. I shall find you, wherever you may hide."

Arsinoe stared at her reflection in the mirror and smoothed her hair. Dee's body felt so alive, vibrant, healthy. Strange that the gods had willed that she retain her host's features and not revert to her own. Strange, too, that she was so aware of Dee's spirit within her body. Not in control, but a presence nonetheless. She seemed tortured, riddled with guilt. But then, she had a lot to feel guilty about.

Arsinoe heard the key scrape in the lock and faced the door.

The sound of a man's footsteps echoed through the hall. The library door opened and a face familiar to Dee smiled at her. Seconds later, he took her in his arms, stroking her hair and kissing her. Dee's spirit yearned for him. Arsinoe let her enjoy his caresses—for the last time.

"Is it done?" Phil asked. "Paula took the pills? I wasn't sure she was convinced she needed help. I knew I hadn't persuaded her she was going out of her mind. But when you told her she had all those suppressed childhood memories, that was a masterstroke. Remind me never to get on the wrong side of you. For real, I mean." He laughed.

Arsinoe, back in control, was beginning to enjoy herself. "It is done. She is gone from here."

Phil's face clouded over. "You mean she's dead, right?"

"To this world."

He looked agitated. "You're remarkably cool about it, Dee. I thought you two were close once."

Arsinoe didn't reply. Inside her, Dee's spirit struggled for control— and failed.

"Where is…where did they take her? They *did* take her, didn't they? I mean, she's not still here, is she?"

"You don't need to worry about that. It is all taken care of."

Phil exhaled. "That's good. I couldn't have gone through a funeral, and as for her body being here…" He shivered.

Arsinoe wouldn't mention the bodies lying in a basement room.

Phil hugged her tight. "Dee, you don't know how long I've waited for this. I thought I'd never be free of her. If it wasn't for her money, we could have been together all along, but now it will all be ours. If your father hadn't cut you out of his will, Paula could still have been alive. It's his fault we had to kill her. It's been so hard pretending to hate you when all I wanted to do was smother you in kisses, but it was worth it. Now we can be together as we always planned."

"I have learned to be patient."

"You played your part well. You were so convincing. I thought, if anything, we went a little too far sometimes, but it only seemed to convince her more."

"And now you have all that you desire."

"And, I hope, so do you." He covered her face with kisses.

Arsinoe endured the attention. After all, it wouldn't be for long. Then she would be free to live anyway she wanted, for as long as this body pleased her.

On the table behind the man, the gold dagger gleamed. Arsinoe smiled at it.

And reached out her hand.

Afterword

Paula swam out of her unconscious state, and Isis surrounded her with a gossamer blanket of peace. She spoke to her. "Come, and I will show you a special place. A place of life and death. Of birth and rebirth…"

Paula floated, carried along by a nebulous wave. All around her, lights flickered red, gold, silver. Her spirit rejoiced. She spoke, her voice a shadowy echo. "What is this place?"

The soothing tones of her companion wafted over her. "A place you were always meant to be."

Paula lifted her arms and saw they were transparent, and it was right somehow. Her new skin glowed, pulsed with life. A new life. A life that shouldn't be. Couldn't be… The lights flickered once and went out. The soft whispers silenced. Isis transformed into a figure of evil. Trickery. That mistress of deceit—Arsinoe—had triumphed. Fooled her into thinking Isis protected her.

Arsinoe laughed at Paula's anguish as the darkness descended over her once more. She lifted her arms and cried out to the interminable blackness that surrounded her. Paula touched her face and felt only scaly, flaky skin. A sudden burst of white light showed that her hands were scorched and blackened, skeletal.

"Help me!"

"You are beyond help now." Arsinoe's voiced echoed all around her. "The price you must pay to keep my faithless sister trapped in a world not of her choosing."

"*Please…*"

But only silence replied. Arsinoe had left her alone. Paula closed her eyes. The white light snapped off.

But she could sense someone.

Out there in the darkness of eternity.

Hands grasped her shoulders, tugging her back, dragging her down through the shaft of light. Terror seized every nerve and muscle. Paralyzed her so she couldn't fight.

Her voice—now no more than a cracked whisper. "Who are you?"

Shadows swirled and an icy breeze froze her soul.

Acknowledgments

Many thanks, as always, to my friend and fellow author, Julia Kavan for all her help and advice on an earlier draft of this. Her guidance has prevented many an unforgivable lapse in judgment, direction, plot and much, much more.

Thank you to all my writer friends, including The Shippy Writers. We meet every month in Liverpool—a small but perfectly formed and diverse group currently composed of people who enjoy writing scary stories. Other genres are welcome!

Massive thanks also to 'The Two Davids' at Crossroad Press for their support and for being such a brilliant publisher.

And to you—thank you for reading. It would be awfully quiet around here without you. Quintillus will return (well, you knew that, didn't you?

About the Author

Following a varied career in sales, advertising and career guidance, Catherine Cavendish is now the full-time author of a number of paranormal, ghostly and Gothic horror novels and novellas.

Her novels include: *The Stones of Landane*, *Those Who Dwell in Mordenhyrst Hall*, *The After-Death of Caroline Rand*, *Nemesis of the Gods* trilogy: *Wrath of the Ancients*, *Waking the Ancients*, and *Damned by the Ancients*, *Dark Observation*, *In Darkness, Shadows Breathe*, *The Garden of Bewitchment*. *The Haunting of Henderson Close*, *The Devil's Serenade*, *The Pendle Curse* and *Saving Grace Devine*.

The Crow Witch and Other Conjurings is a collection of her previously published and brand new short stories.

Her novellas include: *The Darkest Veil*, *Linden Manor*, *Cold Revenge*, *Miss Abigail's Room*, *The Demons of Cambian Street*, *Dark Avenging Angel*, *The Devil Inside Her*, and *The Second Wife*.

She lives by the sea in Southport, England with her long-suffering husband, and a black cat called Serafina who has never forgotten that her species used to be worshipped in ancient Egypt. She sees no reason why that practice should not continue.

You can connect with Cat here:

Website: catherinecavendish.com/
Facebook: facebook.com/CatherineCavendishWriter
X (formerly Twitter): twitter.com/Cat_Cavendish
Instagram: instagram.com/catcavendish/
Tik Tok: catcavendish
Bluesky @catcavendish.bsky.social

Curious about other Crossroad Press books? Stop by our website: http://crossroadpress.com

We offer quality writing

in digital, audio, and print formats.

Subscribe to our newsletter on the website homepage and receive a free eBook.

www.ingramcontent.com/pod-product-compliance
Lightning Source LLC
Chambersburg PA
CBHW020630180626
46816CB00003B/890